Helen Bea Ki

What Matters Most

Loretta,
my friend -
Happy reading -
H B Kirk
2018

A Novel by

Helen Bea Kirk

Paperback
ISBN: 978069294367
Dallas, Texas

www.hbkirkpublishing.com

Publication Date: 4/23/2017

To Denis and Jenny

Contents

Acknowledgements

This book would not exist if it were not for the amazing cheerleaders in my life. Thank you, family. I love you all. I would be remiss to exclude old bones and cancer. Had it not been for the surgery that knocked me off my feet and into bed, where I took pen in hand, 'What Matters Most', would not have been born. Thank you, old bones and cancer. Thank you, Lord.

1 The Pearls

"I'm so scared. It's hard to believe this is my reality, but this is the way it's got to be. I must get them back." She glanced over at the passenger seat; it wasn't funny, but her pistol was riding shotgun. The deadly, cold, black steel was her partner in the crime she was about to commit. A quick glance in the rear-view mirror confirmed her thoughts; she was unrecognizable. Her shoulder length silky blonde hair was completely covered, and no one would ever guess she had perfectly flawless skin under the layers of cheap Halloween makeup. She was certain that even her gender would be in question in the clothes she chose.

Her quest to bring her loved ones back, piece by piece, began when she was robbed. After the shock of the theft abated, anger filled her; enough to provoke her to hunt. She marched into Ace's pawnshop, not expecting to drain her checking account to buy back her own guns; a pistol and two rifles. Her indignation swelled to outrage over the transaction. Having her precious possessions stolen from her, and then having to buy them back, felt like choosing to lie down on a bed of nails. But, it had to be done. She and Paxton had purchased those guns. He'd taken her to gun ranges numerous times and she always looked forward to it. After he was assigned overseas,

Meagan continued shooting frequently. Successfully recouping the weapons, empowered her. She was physically strong, but a gun changed the equation; it added to her bravado and propelled her to King's Pawnshop that evening.

The East Valley shopping center buzzed with activity. A popular Italian restaurant was the biggest draw. She rolled to a stop several shops away from King's Pawn and hopped out of Paxton's unremarkable, brown, Dodge Ram truck.

There was no room for doubt. She was running on instinct, which told her that if she looked for her belongings, she would find them. As she approached the building, she fully expected to encounter another vestige of her life. The anticipation of the reunion was making her jittery.

She was in luck; the door wasn't locked. The sign on the door of King's Pawn stated they closed three minutes ago; Meagan took a deep breath and pushed the door open with authority. Surprised, the shopkeeper quickly muted the country music blaring from his cell phone. "We're closed," he stated.

When she devised her crucial scheme for justice, she knew it would require the diligence of a soldier to conceal her identity. She accomplished it. Meagan wore Paxton's army fatigues, tucked into the black, well worn, army issued boots he had died in. They felt good on her feet. His leather jacket hung awkwardly on her slim figure, revealing his AC/DC rock band t-shirt.

His curiosity was piqued as he expertly wrapped up counting the till and zipped the cash bag shut. He checked his Breitling wristwatch and sucked in a deep breath while the pseudo-military hobo surveyed the guitars for sale. Ordinarily, King would have gladly assisted a late pawn customer, but tonight he had planned to talk to Gayla. It was a long overdue conversation.

King raced back to his office to toss the cash bag in the vault. Storm's growl caused him to hurry back to his customer in the front of the store.

He couldn't see the eyes; the aviator sunglasses were too dark. The hair was obscured and concealed under a black knit cap. Brown lipstick and fake, blue plastic dentures masked her lips and teeth.

King noticed every detail about the tall vagabond as she paced his shop. Her makeup was severe and overdone—almost comical. He knew she was protecting her identity with someone else's wardrobe. Without much history or understanding of women, King Pullman's insight into people emanated from his eight years in the pawn business. If he were a betting man, he would have laid odds she wasn't shopping, she was prowling; doing recon. His stomach flipped at the thought.

She stood erect; shoulders squared and met King's calm hazel eyes. "I'm looking for some jewelry."

"What we have is all here." He gestured to the long display case before him.

Meagan noted the minor differences between this shop and the shop she visited several days before. The other store was a bit smaller than King's Pawn and didn't smell as good. As she neared the bearded gentleman behind the counter, she recognized the pleasant, woodsy scent was coming from him. He smelled inviting and familiar, like green tea and spice cake in a forest. A distant memory of her uncle Abe's tobacco pipe floated to mind.

"Would you like to see something in here?" the broad-chested man inquired, causing her to snap back to the present.

Her eyes darted to the imposing German Shepherd lying on the floor behind the pleasant-smelling man. His growl escalated as she drew near.

"Storm! Hush!" the man commanded, silencing the dog. He kept his eye on the suspiciously costumed person as she examined a photo in her hand. Even upside down, King could identify the gems in the snap-shot. She was undeniably doing reconnaissance. Nothing good had ever come from a customer's discovery of their former possessions in his store.

Things were not going well.

It was a rotten time for King to recall asking Marty to fix the silent alarm button. Screws had loosened, and the button—- once attached to the back of the counter—lay inconveniently on the floor, in the corner, under the cabinet.

"They have to be here," she muttered under her breath, although there was no sign of the amber ring. The white gold band with four prongs grasping the solitary, stunning amber stone, was given to her by her father upon his mother's death. She studied the assortment of jewelry inside the sizeable glass case. Meagan hoped her Grandmother Pearl's signature necklace would be there too.

"Could I see those?" She pointed to the tray containing a string of pearls, and then tucked her hand back in her jacket pocket.

King took the cabinet key from his jeans' pocket, unlocked the sliding glass panels, and then set the tray of jewels on the counter while assessing her body language. The moment she examined them, he knew she was locked on the pearls.

"If you haven't been in here before," he coached, "how it works is, you tell me a price you are willing to pay, and we negotiate."

She was momentarily paralyzed by her emotions; elated by the discovery of the pearls and disgusted there was only one Morris family heirloom in the shop. No ruby rose brooch or cameo; no amber ring, opal choker, or pocket-watch; and clearly, no painting or pheasant, speed bag or guitar. She would have to hunt harder.

The moment of peril arrived.

"Hands up! Right, now!" she ordered, extracting the 9-mm handgun from the pocket of Pax's leather jacket. "I will shoot you, so don't do anything stupid."

As Storm sailed over the counter like a track hurdler, King shouted, "Stand down!" Storm's toenails skidded across the smooth cement floor before he froze in his tracks—watching Meagan like prey. King worried his nervous assailant might panic and shoot his dog. Meagan flashed the gun from King to the dog and back to King. The thought of anyone injuring Storm made King's heart race.

"Shooting me would be stupid, don't you think?" he said, lifting his hands in the air. He eyed the alarm button and stretched his leg out as far as he could without falling, and then stretched... just a bit ... more.

"What are you doing?" Meagan demanded in her deepest voice. As she lurched forward to see what he was doing behind the counter, Storm grabbed the seat of her baggy pants and jerked her backward. As she stumbled, she accidentally fired the gun, leaving a new hole in the ceiling.

"Shit," King growled and hit the small round alarm button with the toe of his cowboy boot. He would discuss shop repairs with Marty, later, and point out the new hole in the roof. The triggered alarm was linked to the police station; they were likely already on their way. "Stand down, Storm."

The second she was free of the dog's grip, Meagan scrambled to the counter; her gloved fingers still wrapped around the pistol. She resumed pointing the gun at King's chest and he re-hoisted his hands into the air.

With her free hand, Meagan felt the back of the old camo pants, looking for holes. King tried to hide a smirk and was on the verge of snickering at her. This had to be a woman, the way she yelped when Storm jerked her back and then the way she checked her clothing. "Now, where were we?" he asked her. "Oh, yes, I think you were robbing me."

Meagan glared at the dark-haired, handsome man and was not amused. She pulled the plastic grocery store sack out of her back pocket. With the gun leveled on him, she plucked the long strand of pearls off the tray, and with a gentle hand, dropped it into her flimsy bag. The almost-botched plan was now back on track. She was elated.

Then she wasn't.

"I'm outta here," Meagan announced and slung the bag off the counter with a cocky fling of her head, sending the pearls flying across the shop. "No!" she yelled. "No!" Storm's teeth had punctured the flimsy sack.

Officer Dell and the Pullman family were well acquainted and had maintained a good working relationship over the years… one that included 'no light bar warning lights.' Dell stealthily swung the cruiser into the parking lot near King's Pawn. It amazed him that King and his family were still in the pawn business after all these years. "Those Pullman men must be made of grit to put up with all the nonsense," he mused. A reality television show filmed in their shops would have made them millionaires because most people love a good crime drama.

The parking lot was still teeming with cars, which made seeking out King's robber more difficult. As far as Dell was concerned, the most suspicious vehicle was a brown truck with a mud-obscured license plate. "Par for the course," he muttered as he checked to ensure he had all the equipment he might need.

The evening was cool and overcast when Dell closed the cruiser door and glanced over once more at the brown truck; a reflective sticker on the back window read, 'Girls love trucks too!' "Hmm," Dell mumbled. The brilliant LED headlights of the cruiser flooded the shop, reflecting off the hanging brass musical instruments. Dell had inadvertently announced his arrival.

Meagan froze like a deer in headlights. She was positive she was going to jail. Feeling like she had nothing to lose, she threatened through clenched teeth, "I want my pearls. You get them, or I'll shoot your hand!"

"You'll... what?" King wondered if he understood her correctly. He glanced at his currently intact palms and fingers. Why someone would target one of his hands was a mystery to him. He could swear he heard her heart pounding. The only people he had ever seen sweat like this criminal were drug addicts. Suddenly, he felt like there was going to be a fatality in his shop.

"Storm, fetch!" King commanded. His dog obeyed and bolted for the pearls that dangled from the handlebar of a racing bike.

Dell had handcuffed his fair share of women in his career. He recalled yanking two hookers out of King's Pawn not too long ago. That had been a rough one for Dell. Those women were so nice to him; absolutely the most pleasant and flirtatious criminals he had ever met. Maybe this wouldn't go so badly—if it were a woman—again. He smiled, sometimes his job was a piece of cake.

The moment the door flew open and Dell entered, pointing his gun toward Meagan, she shoved hers back in her pocket.

"Officer Delbert Wims! Put your hands up!" he bellowed.

"Hi, Dell," King greeted the friendly, black officer. "You just missed him. Black truck, Hispanic or Brazilian, I couldn't tell. He took off with an iPhone," King lied smoothly and gently took the pearls from Storm's mouth; patting his head. "Good boy."

Meagan's heart dropped to her stomach and pounded harder than ever, as she imagined she was about to be taken into custody. Her head felt like it was on fire and sweat trickled down her neck from under the knit cap. Her armpits were swimming. She thought about running but imagined getting shot in the back. Grandma Pearl would have hated that. She would have given Meagan a sweet, but stern, lecture on the pitfalls of stealing and running from the police. Her breathing was shallow as she listened to the two men and concentrated on not fainting.

The man behind the counter picked up Meagan's pearls, casually wiped off the dog slobber and deposited them into a King's Pawn bag; as though she purchased them. "Doubt you'll catch him, he had friends waiting," he told the officer.

Meagan was dumbfounded as she watched him toss in a jewelry case for the pearls.

Dell knew it only took him five minutes to get to the shop. "Oh, so everything is fine?" he checked; baffled that he missed the culprit. He scratched his chin and stared at the lanky customer, suspiciously.

"Here you go. Come back and see me," King instructed, handing the bag to Meagan.

She hoped that no one could see the humiliation heating her cheeks under all her makeup. "Thank you. Excuse me," she whispered, averting her Halloween face and gratefully slipping past the officer at the door.

"Hmm," Dell mumbled and stepped aside, holding the door open for her.

King glanced down and hastily grabbed the photo the robber left behind. He would study it later. For the time being, it fit nicely in the breast pocket of his buttoned-down shirt.

"These kids, Dell, they think we owe them everything. It makes me want to retire."

"I know what you mean." Dell poured himself a cup of coffee and turned the pot off. "How much did that punk get away with?"

"About two hundred dollars."

Officer Dell slurped his coffee and strolled toward the exit. "Sorry I didn't make it in time, King. That man, the one who just left, has he been in here before?"

"Do you mean 'him'?" King asked pointing to the shop door. "No. I thought it was a woman. Strange person, but I try not to let that influence the deal."

Dell laughed when he realized he had jumped to conclusions about the truck and the customer. He was positive the alarm call had been for the bum in King's shop. "Strange fella."

King agreed, "Yes, strange."

"Yeah but ignoring the way someone looks would be hard though," Dell commented. "Why'd you get into this business, King? Seems like there are better, I mean, safer things you could do."

"I appreciate your concern, Dell. This business gives me the freedom I need to do other things. Besides, you know that I carry a gun and I know how to use it if I ever needed to." His lips formed a thin smile at his trusty friend. He was anxious for Dell to leave so he could examine the photo more carefully. The decision to blow off a potentially ugly talk with Gayla was simple considering his near-death robbery experience.

"Okay, then," Officer Dell conceded, "I'm glad you're okay.

"Thanks, Dell."

King bolted the glass and iron door after Officer Dell and killed the lights on his way to the back office to study the picture.

Only the hum of the air filter motor could be heard. The shop was eerily quiet as he settled into his rustic wooden banker's chair and put on a pair of his dad's old, round, reading glasses. King refused to let on to anyone that his vision was not perfect anymore. He knew it was silly, but he didn't read anything small if other people were around. Thankfully, his manager, Marty hadn't noticed the increased font size on his cell phone, he would have been the butt of Marty's jokes forever.

"Hmm," King muttered. If he had to guess, he'd say the people in the photo were likely relatives of the robber. A little girl, about four years old in the photo, wore a fancy amber ring on her thumb; it was mounted high and appeared expensive. Peering through the large magnifying glass vice-gripped to his desk, he confirmed the thief took the pearls worn by the eldest woman. If the thief was after anything else in this photo, King concluded it would have been a ruby rose brooch, two necklaces, and that amber ring. He knew he should check the inventory at his brother's shop and his dad's as well. With his mother in the hospital, the last thing the Pullman family needed was a homicide because of a deranged person in military dress-up.

Meagan struggled with her emotions. Twenty-four miles to the B and B passed in a blur after the shock of her robbery-turned-gift. Tears threatened to spill over because of the kindness the big man exhibited. She wished she understood his reasoning. He had every right to hand her over to the cop. She groped around in the sack and... no photo.

Luckily, the thieves who ruined her life had not destroyed her family photo album, the only place her loved ones still resided. She had plenty of other pictures.

Dragging herself up the creaking stairs to her third-floor room in the lovely Victorian home, she recalled two weeks earlier. It had been a stressful day at work and she was looking forward to changing clothes and working out in the gym. When she rounded the corner to her apartment, she knew something horrible had happened. She pushed aside the destroyed front door to the shock and horror of being robbed. Strange, how radically her life changed at that moment.

Since Paxton's death, Meagan had not felt comfortable in their home. That was odd, because while he was alive, she spent most of her time alone in the house. Knowing she was 'manning the homestead' while her husband fought had been her mission throughout their ten-year marriage. After he died, it worked for a year—then she went broke.

Massaging her temples with her thumbs, she tried to erase the image of her trashed apartment and the zeros in her bank account. Tomorrow, after work, she would hunt again. Since her job at the Appliance Warehouse did not allow her time to surf the Internet for her belongings, she planned to use the computers in the city library.

2 Secrets

King received a text from Ace, "Shit, Mom is in a coma."

Rather than respond with a text, he dialed his younger brother. "How's she doing? Ace, I called you early this morning for an explanation. Why didn't you answer?"

"Yeah, I overslept. Late night. Doc says it's probably not permanent. Dad is pretty calm about the whole thing."

The bizarrely teenage behavior from twenty-eight-year-old Ace was bewildering to King, but he decided not to interrogate his brother just yet. "Mom is going to be fine. It will just take longer than we thought. I have to ask you about a customer."

"Shoot."

"She's a clown-looking woman with dark glasses, fake teeth, and wearing military garb," King recalled. The more he reconstructed her in his head, the more he realized if he or she had been buying car parts, King would have assumed the thief was male. Embarrassed, he cleared his throat. "Actually, it could have been a guy ... with a soft voice."

Ace coughed to cover his snickers. "What happened? Your love life sucks so bad you're going after customers now?"

"Smart ass! Only the ones who rob me."

"You were robbed? What?" snapped Ace. "There was a guy by that description—at least I think it was a guy. He came in a couple of days back and bought guns; two rifles and a pistol. He knew what he wanted, and he paid."

Surprised, King asked, "How did you do on the deal?"

"I made triple what I paid for them." Ace's phone beeped with another call. "I gotta go, bro. Tell Mom and Dad hi for me. Sorry you got taken, dude."

"Thanks, I'll do that." King set his cell phone in the console cup holder and stared blankly at the rush hour traffic, contemplating his day. Yeah, a shirt and tie desk-job career would have been fine ... for anyone but King. It seemed to him his finance professors expected him to be able to whip a necktie into a Full Windsor Knot and claim his desk, shortly after graduation.

Growing up Pullman meant freedom, cattle, and land; not, office, housecat, and condo. Besides, he wasn't interested in learning the fifteen different ways to knot a necktie and choke the life out of himself.

The traffic light turned green and King proceeded to the hospital parking lot. He tugged at the crew neck of the t-shirt under his plaid buttoned-down shirt and headed for the elevator.

At the end of the sterile hospital corridor, he slipped into his mother's room. "Hey Dad, how's Mom doing?" he whispered, entering the dimly lit space.

"She's in a coma, son. The doc said it's the brain's way of dealing with a stroke sometimes. Her sister is coming to sit with her, so I can work the rest of the week."

King kissed his mother on the forehead and settled into a hard, metal hospital chair beside his father. His heart ached for his kind and strong mother; she appeared more frail than he had ever seen her. "Yeah, I need to talk to you about that, Dad. Beware of a person dressed in camo fatigues and military issued boots. She'll rob you," he stated, then closed his eyes to pray for his mother.

"Was Dell working?" inquired Jack.

"Yes, but I couldn't hand her over to a cop. Damnedest thing. I just couldn't do it. Maybe I've gone soft, Dad. I just let her take the shit." He omitted the part about being at gunpoint and silently chided himself for labeling the thief a woman.

Jack's eyebrows rose as he surveyed his eldest son with surprise. "That's a new one. I remember when Dell hauled those two strippers out of your shop. You handed them over with no questions; didn't give them a chance. They were good looking and throwing themselves at you. Geez, now, you've gone Greenpeace on everyone. What's going on?"

"Not sure," King responded to the ceiling, slunk down in the chair, head tilted back, legs straight out and crossed at the ankles. "I'll figure it out though. It won't happen again." Somehow, King knew—because he felt it in his gut—she wouldn't be back. Ace's Pawn and King's Pawn were just stops on her way. "She's dangerous," King warned again, yawning.

Jack assured his son, "I'll call Mr. Lee, tomorrow."

King suspected the heist did not surprise his dad. It seemed to him that ever since he purchased the ranch from his parents several years ago, bizarre things kept happening.

Irish through and through, Jack Pullman was a devilishly handsome, but superstitious man and his family knew it well. King had overheard his parents talking one evening. Jack was doing his best to talk Brenda into selling that bad-luck, cracker box house they called a garden home and getting some real land again.

King refused to say it out loud, but he knew he had to protect his dad. If soldier girl were to shove a gun in Jack's face, she wouldn't last long. Jack was known for his quick, brutal temper, which if confronted by the pissed off woman who robbed King, could be a lethal combination. King could not let that happen, for both their sakes. He patted the pocket containing the robber's photo to make sure it was still there before drifting off to sleep. "She's bad news. You need Storm."

"Hmm mm," Jack acknowledged, assuming the same posture as his son. They fell awkwardly asleep in their chairs at the side of Brenda Pullman's bed.

It was one a.m. on a Thursday. Ten-year-old Meagan was spending the night at Rhonda's house when her parents received the phone call that shattered Meagan's world. Mr. and Mrs. Morris died in a small, single engine plane crash less than seventy-five miles from town. With the loss of her parents, Rhonda became possessive of Meagan, like a momma cat trying to protect her kitten from the harsh universe; it was a gallant effort.

Meagan learned to be tough. She had been a princess, once, but her reign ended with the death of her tender, loving parents. They were the sweetest, most thoughtful people on earth. At their funerals people came out of the woodwork to speak about them and their kindness.

Her years since their passing had been filled with work and punctuated with stretches of loneliness and introversion. Looking back on it, Meagan recognized her parent's absence came at a pivotal point in her life when she struggled for self-assurance and love. She often gazed into the bathroom mirror, longing for the warmth of loving arms around her, and wondered if anyone would ever love her again.

Always bubbly and on her phone, Rhonda consistently invited Meagan along with friends. Sometimes, she went; most of the time, she stayed home alone in the bedroom at the opposite end of the hall from Rhonda's. She spent hours by herself. With sheets of music spread out all over the bed, Meagan taught herself to play the acoustic guitar her uncle, Abe Morris, had bequeathed to her.

Rhonda was by Meagan's side when her grandmother, Pearl, passed, and then her aunt, Opal. The girls stayed close through middle school and high school.

Marriage, college, and jobs took them separate directions, and they hardly kept in touch. Getting together once a week for lunch began after Paxton's funeral. Rhonda heard on the news Meagan's husband died in Afghanistan. She called her immediately to offer sympathy, and their sisterhood resumed like it had never faltered.

Rhonda followed Meagan to a table on the patio, in the sun. The waiter set two glasses of water before them. "I'll be right back with your teas," he informed them and handed them each a menu before heading back into Banger's Bistro.

"Does the feeling of being violated ever end?" Meagan wondered aloud, half to her friend and half to herself.

Rhonda sighed. "You mean, about your robbery? I don't think so, Meagan. Eventually, it just won't be so raw. Right now, you should focus on work and rebuilding your life. I wish you had rented an apartment with security gates."

"Yeah, well. I was flat broke and couldn't afford a fancy place. Now I'm broker... if that's even possible!" She rolled her eyes in disgust.

After Paxton's death, Meagan held on to their house until it ate up her savings and she was forced to sell it. She lived in her cheap apartment for less than two weeks when the robbery occurred. What wasn't stolen was broken.

Refusing to rent another unit in the same complex, she reached out to her deceased father's second cousin, Agnes Willowby. Agnes and her husband owned the

Willowby Bed and Breakfast. She was a nosy woman Meagan met once when she was twelve and again at Paxton's funeral.

The Bistro waiter set cups of hot tea before them and took their menus. The breeze kicked up, tossing Rhonda's brilliant red hair around like flames licking at the air. "Two soups of the day with crusty bread, please," she ordered and scraped wild hair strands away from her mouth, frustrated.

"Just put your hair in a clip, Rhonda," Meagan advised. "See." She shook her own ponytail. "It works." She loved getting out of her cramped corner office at Appliance Warehouse and having lunch outside when the weather was decent.

"How's your crazy aunt Agnes?" Rhonda inquired, trapping her hair behind her ears.

"She's snoopy, as usual. She keeps asking me why I'm single, and yesterday she introduced me to her son, Andrew. I didn't remember him. It was... weird." Meagan thought it was a strange introduction because she didn't remember Andrew at any holiday get-togethers when her family was alive. Even weirder was the age gap; Mr. and Mrs. Willowby had to have been at least fifty-years-old when Andrew was born.

Rhonda's eyes widened. "How old is Andrew? Does he live there too? Across the hall, maybe? Is he hot? Why are you laughing?"

"He travels for work, but he lives there—on the second floor," Meagan snickered, "and no, he's not hot; warm at best and thirty-ish. You know me!"

Rhonda nodded; her radiant locks still dancing in the afternoon breeze. "Yes, I do know you! Unless he is super smart, has buns of steel and abs of iron, along with perfect teeth and ..." she listed.

"Wait a minute, I'm not that bad," Meagan argued defensively. "Really, Rhonda? Am I that shallow?"

"I'm supposed to answer that?" the waiter teased, snickering. He set their soup dishes down. "I just serve food."

"You are wise. Incredibly wise," Rhonda informed the clean-shaven young man. "How old are you?" She took a bite.

"I'm twenty-seven. I have been told I have a baby face," he replied with a smile.

Rhonda's cheeks protruded like a chipmunk's as she glared at him. Meagan began to giggle. She knew when Rhonda first laid eyes on the waiter, she thought of him like a child. Twenty-seven was a game changer, so Rhonda was evaluating him as a potential bedmate... or so it seemed to Meagan. The waiter must have felt the heat of Rhonda's stare because he all but ran back into the restaurant.

Rhonda shrugged and muttered, "Coward!" causing Meagan to choke with laughter at her old friend's desperation for a man. She swallowed her food and resumed the earlier subject. "No, you're not shallow, Meagan, I think that may be part of your problem. I've known you practically all your life and I'm still trying to figure you out. I don't want to sound 'preachy', but I feel like you're keeping secrets, Meg, and we said we would never do that." Rhonda's face softened sadly. "We were each other's maid of honor, remember? Even though you're a widow and I'm divorced, we're still 'maids of honor.' We have our code, right?"

"I have a lot of stuff... in my head, that I'm processing," Meagan replied and smiled weakly. "I don't mean to seem secretive. I'm sorry. Are we still good for Saturday night?"

"Absolutely, my mom is babysitting Alex, so we can try that new bar. I've heard it's fun. See you then?" she checked.

"Yes, thanks for understanding."

A ripple of guilt ran through Meagan as she recalled her decade-long marriage to Paxton Calvert. Each Army mission had changed him and altered his sense of humor and tolerance. He lost his compassion and became progressively more competitive with Meagan. He had to be right, and she had to be wrong. He had to be the faster runner, the superior breadwinner, and the stronger puncher.

When their next-door neighbor offered Meagan a job, earning more money than Paxton, she turned it down to keep the peace in her marriage.

If Rhonda had ever been privy to the inner workings of Meagan's marriage, she would have thought Meagan was crazy and urged her to divorce. How do you tell your best friend you're comfortable with a man who rarely talks to you, seems peeved at you all the time, and tells you to shut up if you sing?

After Pax's death, their renewed friendship was a lifeline to Meagan because Rhonda was a critical link to her youth. The rock she had always clung to, however, was her 'stuff.' Those cherished items handed down to her by her grandparents, her aunts, and her parents—she needed them most. The memory of the priceless gifts that were stolen from her fed her fire. The possibility of never seeing them again was unfathomable. Telling Rhonda that seemed equally impossible. So, she would continue hunting. When all her possessions were home, maybe then, she would confess her mission to Rhonda.

3 Naked and Waiting

Late evening, after leaving the hospital, King returned to his shop to pick up Storm then stopped at his dad's pawnshop on his way home. All three Pullman men had keys to each other's pawn businesses in case of an emergency. King believed zero hour had arrived.

He flipped on a couple of lights. Studying the photo from his breast pocket, he scanned his dad's display cabinet for the remaining jewelry pieces his assailant hadn't found in his shop.

He hit pay dirt when he spotted the cameo pendant on a stunning gold, snake chain. "Shit. She'll definitely want this," he said, comparing it to the piece in the photo. King figured if the coral and ivory cameo necklace were not there, she would just leave Jack's shop peacefully, without burglarizing him. Leafing through his wallet, he placed three one-hundred-dollar bills in a cash drop bag with a note for Jack, or his manager, Mr. Lee. "Let me know if this doesn't cover the gold chain necklace with the lady's head pendant, Thanks, B.K.P."

By three thirty in the morning, King was exhausted as he idled up his gravel driveway. Frustration furrowed his brow; Gayla's SUV was there. "Damn," he muttered, giving Storm a good petting. "I just wanted to be alone. You know what I'm talking about?" he questioned the dog. King would have preferred to wallow in his thoughts solo tonight, but he knew she was in his bed; naked and waiting for him.

Ace was up to something, and King needed time to think about his brother. His mother hospitalized and, in a coma, weighed on him too. He worried about his dad. His parents were each other's world. King was also woefully behind on his second-floor building project and craved time to swing a hammer. He tried not to give his jewelry thief any thought, but his mind saw her clearly and imagined ten different possible actions he could have taken during the robbery. Most of the scenarios ended with the tall woman behind bars, leaving him feeling very conflicted.

Once again, he decided to stall the inevitable necessary talk with Gayla. "Let's go," he ordered Storm, and they marched into the house. He dropped his clothes in a pile and fell into bed. Storm swaggered over to his massive dog bed in the corner of the bedroom and curled up for the night.

"Hey babe," Gayla cooed in her raspy voice. "Where have you been?"

"Visiting my parents."

"Oh." Her fingers combed his chest. "Let's forget our day for a while."

Although Gayla's scent had never aroused King, her touch still worked. Her skin generally reeked like the counter top antiseptic spray she used at her clinic, other times, she smelled like rhubarb and tobacco. She was needy and gave sex for the false reassurance of a future with King. It had always been like that for them. He held her sinewy form on top of him and studied her.

"You need to let go and escape your head, babe," she told him. "If you want to play the head game, I can tell you about the horse I put down today. The family stood around telling stories about his damn life for an hour before they let me inject him. They were crying and carrying on. I thought they'd never stop. Poor horse, when he finally stopped breathing, guess what happened?"

King shook his head in disbelief that Gayla was talking a blue streak while they had sex, but hell, he took it. It was better than listening to her when they weren't having sex.

"What?"

"This dog, an old Brittany Spaniel, walks up to the dead Mustang, licks his face, lies on him, and starts whining. That shit is so sad, you know?" she asked, picking up the rhythm. "My brother is gone again, so I need money. Can you give me some?"

"Uh huh," King muttered while pumping numbly, like a piston engine on autopilot.

For a veterinarian with her own practice, Gayla continually ran short on money. It was something King had been avoiding confronting her about, and his checkbook reflected it. But push was coming to shove, despite their entangled past.

Their entangled past.

Gayla's family moved into the farmhouse a half-mile down the road when she was in the eighth grade and he was in the ninth. In a matter of weeks, Gayla developed a crush on King. She sat quietly near him on the school bus every day and fantasized being kissed by him. When she pulled her head out of the clouds, she was content if he said, "hello" to her.

King's junior year in high school, he and Ace threw a Halloween bonfire party on their property. Practically the entire school attended; over three hundred kids ate s'mores and danced in the field. There were those few who smuggled in alcohol and drank too much. When King thought back on that night, alcohol must have been a factor in what happened to Gayla. He would never forget it.

Mr. and Mrs. Pullman patrolled and chaperoned the bonfire party, but they were not enough. King was buzzed from a half pint of some spiked concoction that smelled of rum. A couple of his friends asked if he wouldn't mind telling Gayla Adamson about the karaoke party in the barn. The athletic, gangly, seventeen-year-old King did exactly that, and Gayla was receptive.

"Only if you'll come with me," she urged.

"Sure," King slurred, "in a bit. I have to use the bathroom."

She wandered to the barn alone.

Later, when he noticed people leaving the party and jogging to their cars, he remembered Gayla. He guessed something was amiss before he got to the barn. Kids were still screeching out rock song lyrics into the karaoke mike while King began frantically searching for Gayla. He found her hidden among carefully stacked piles of hay bales.

"I thought you'd never get here," she breathed through her puffy, busted lip. "Your friend had sex with me. It wasn't all it's cracked up to be," she whined through her tears. She was lying on a bale of hay, her blouse torn, her jeans and underwear cast aside.

A lump formed in King's throat, blocking the vomit that threatened to erupt. "Assholes," was all he could think to say as he helped Gayla to her feet. He tried, but failed, to recall the faces of those who had requested her. Gayla remained adamant in her assertion that someone kept her eyes covered, so she didn't see who defiled her.

"My back hurts," she said.

"Gayla, you're bleeding!" King was shocked at the deep scratches the hay etched into her back and buttocks. He removed his shirt and wrapped it around her then helped her step into her panties and jeans.

"I can't believe I wanted to have sex with you all these years. It's awful," she sobbed.

King was aghast at the news of her desire for him. "Well, I don't think it's supposed to be," he confided. "Come to the house and I can help clean your back, but you need to see a doctor."

Jack Pullman whipped the bathroom door open as his eldest son had secured Gayla in an embrace. King was facing the mirror and tending to her back wounds while she wept on his naked chest. Jack never saw her face. He was enraged. "You have five seconds to get dressed and get her the hell home."

Gayla apologized to King for involving him in her situation but blamed him because he hosted the party. If he hadn't thrown the party, she wouldn't have had sex. King and his parents never spoke of the incident, but it troubled King. He began meeting Gayla in a remote spot on her land, behind a workshop. She wanted to know about the sex King claimed didn't hurt. So, it began; King learned about sex by trying to make it gentle for Gayla. Only a month later, he noticed her body changing rapidly and at seventeen-years-old, she admitted she was pregnant with his baby. To her family, however, she told another story. The third rendition of her story, she covertly told Conroy's father. Mr. Sabeth was disgusted that his son, Conroy, was the father of her child. Gayla told him if they didn't want anything to do with the baby, he could pay her forty thousand dollars and be done with it. He would never have to deal with the child.

When Mr. Sabeth saw the baby and learned of the neurological problems that would plague the child throughout his life, he quickly wrote a check and forbade Conroy from speaking to Gayla. Mr. Sabeth and his wife never spoke of the child after that.

King had a motorcycle and worked a weekend job. Upon learning the news he was a father, he picked up more hours and discreetly gave Gayla all the money he could. He managed to keep his grades high but could no longer play sports. There was no time for games, he needed to be a decent provider for his secret child, Gary. He had the impression Gayla was hiding something from him, even before he left for college.

Only twice did Gayla bring baby Gary to her and King's meeting spot by the shed. King laid eyes on the child once before he left for college and once when he got back. In King's estimation, Gayla was the epitome of protectiveness and secretiveness regarding their child. When Gary was young, King asked to take him to a water park and Gayla said no and wouldn't talk about it. There were numerous times King requested time with Gary and each time Gayla refused to allow it. She never had a reasonable excuse.

Gayla's mother and younger brother often took care of Gary. When Gayla went to college to become a veterinarian, her mother and brother stepped in to care for him, full-time.

King was already a year ahead of Gayla and attending college in the neighboring state of Kentucky. He had accepted an academic scholarship for math.

The entire 'baby Gary' puzzle was like a festering sore. He promised himself that after college graduation, when he had enough money, he would hire a lawyer and straighten the mess out.

Ace was starting up his own pawnshop with Jack's help and he was about to buy a house when King was a junior in college. King was impressed with the pawn business, and after looking over Jack's books, he knew he could earn a good living. Bottom line; Ace was making money and King needed to as well, so he jumped on the opportunity. He changed his major from math to business when Jack offered to guide him in the operation of his own pawnshop after graduation.

Conroy Sabeth had emerged from college a lawyer, much to everyone's shock. King needed an attorney to process his purchase of his parent's house and called upon Conroy, at Sabeth and Sabeth Law.

"Yeah, I can help you with that," assured the cocky counselor, "then we'll play some golf."

After King signed the papers, the two men played eighteen holes and a twelve-pack on a sunny afternoon. As luck would have it, his tongue loosened with alcohol, Conroy Sabeth spilled the beans. King learned that Gary was Conroy's child and that his father had paid Gayla off.

"I didn't even know I had a kid, King! I found out two years ago, when I was going through some of Dad's paperwork. When the shock wore off, I was pissed at my dad for intervening."

Conroy talked a good line, but Conroy was all about Conroy. Trying to imagine him with a child was like pigs flying.

King changed that day. The information liberated him emotionally. Gayla was no longer a 'have to' accessory in his bed, but rather a convenient repository for his needs. So long as she didn't hang around for breakfast, he could put up with her shenanigans.

4 The Television

King woke to find that Gayla was gone, as usual. It was an understanding they had. Gayla felt positive that, with time, King would realize her value and want to keep her around longer. She still didn't linger, however, and King preferred it that way.

Meagan had been at the library since the doors opened three hours earlier. She intended to locate more of her property on Drakeslist. Her relentless search for her belongings finally produced something. In the category of 'electronics', she found her television and the surround sound components Paxton had carefully installed in their home.

She texted the seller, "Hi, I'm interested. What year is this TV? Can I see it today?"

Moments later, a response came, "About four-years-old. Yes, we can meet. I'm in Chartville."

Google Earth was helpful as she selected a remote spot for the meeting. "How about the abandoned gas station on Frontage Road at seven p.m.?" she asked.

"We'll be there."

Paxton's face appeared in Meagan's mind; he smiled. A warm feeling of pride enveloped her as she drove home to the B and B. There would be chores to do for Aunt Agnes first, then she could get ready for the meeting. She looked forward to facing the criminals who were attempting to sell her possessions.

Andrew sipped his fourth cup of coffee and slowly raised the old window roller shade. He spied through the crocheted antique curtains as Meagan crossed the parking lot on her way into the B and B. He hurriedly set his coffee cup on the nightstand and hurried downstairs; seizing the opportunity.

"Oh hi," Meagan said, stiffening and eyes wide in surprise.

"Mom told me that you were married," Andrew disclosed. "How old were you when you married?"

"Um, I was eighteen. He died last year."

"I would like to take you to dinner," he informed her.

Meagan began to make her way past Andrew and up the stairs. "Let me think about it. Okay? I need to help Aunt Agnes."

"Oh, right. Okay."

The day after Meagan moved into the B and B, with a nice discount on rent, Aunt Agnes laid down the law. "Mr. Willowby only cooks, so you can help me with the cleaning."

Since Meagan was cornered and doomed to clean, she elected to embrace it. She found vacuuming, dusting, and power washing the walks, patio, and parking lot cathartic. Everything deserved a fresh start in her estimation. Life at the B and B was enlightening. The more she came to understand about the business, the more respect she had for Aunt Agnes and her husband. Being on call twenty-four hours a day took amazing dedication. Mr. and Mrs. Willowby did it all; they booked stay overs, cooked like chefs, and cleaned. They befriended hundreds of people over the years. Successfully managing a bed and breakfast business required an absence of privacy that Meagan could never give up. She was content helping the elderly couple and staying out of the limelight.

By nature, Aunt Agnes was not a quiet person nor complimentary. Oddly, she had been smiling frequently at Meagan lately and it was unsettling.

Mr. Willowby prepared a beautiful Italian Spaghetti dish for dinner, including homemade rolls. Agnes fixed the salad and a Tiramisu for dessert. The atmosphere in the kitchen was tense but exciting for Meagan as she jumped to assist them with their creations.

Growing up in Rhonda's family's home, cooking had never been a priority. Most meals were either takeout or canned soup and hastily made sandwiches. As Meagan got older, she would Google a recipe that made her mouth water and prepare it for the family. In retrospect, if she had grown up in a cooking family, she wouldn't have had time for guitar playing.

Meagan helped Agnes set beautifully arranged plates of food before the guests. A couple visiting from Wisconsin raved about the lovely Italian meal and shared their plans to start a family soon. Meagan enjoyed their conversation while Andrew sat across the table, engrossed in his iPhone.

After dinner, Meagan collected the dishes and cleared the table in anticipation of her Drakeslist meeting. She took a fast shower and threw on sweats. Carefully applying her makeup to the extreme, she rolled up her military ensemble, including boots, into a bag and set out on her quest.

The sun had dropped out of sight hours ago, and Meagan was a mile from her destination. In a gas station bathroom, she changed her clothes and texted the seller of her TV that she was nearby.

"We're already here," they responded.

At the meeting spot, two men waited by a Chevy van. Meagan sized up the surrounding area until she was satisfied no one would see and the coast was clear. She wore the military pants, boots, and leather jacket; the same clothing she sported when she recovered Grandma Pearl's necklace from King's Pawn. Her hair was pulled back in a ponytail and hidden by Paxton's black ball cap instead of the knit cap. The truck's brakes squeaked as she backed it up to their van.

"You military?" asked the taller of the two sellers.

"Yes. I just got back," she lied, "how about you?"

"No. That shit is nuts."

Her hands shoved deep into her pockets, she inquired, "Can I see the TV and equipment?" A brief examination of the equipment confirmed it was hers. "It looks right, does it work?"

"Yes. It works."

Meagan shrugged her shoulders innocently. "Okay, great, but I can't carry it. Can you help?"

"Sure," said the shorter one. They transferred the TV to the bed of Meagan's truck while she hauled the surround sound components. In minutes, her truck was full. She slammed the tailgate in place and turned her gun on them.

"Get the hell out of here before I shoot both of you for selling stolen merchandise!"

"You bitch!" the tall one spat and attempted a front kick. She retaliated by firing her weapon, putting a bullet in the bottom of his foot.

"Damn, what the hell! Jay, get me out of here," he yelled, hopping around. "She fucking shot me!" he cried.

The shorter man helped the bleeding man to their van, and they peeled out of the field. "I'm gonna find you!"

the driver promised and flipped his middle finger at Meagan.

Shaking from the altercation, Meagan climbed behind the wheel, and wiping away tears of stress, she took her TV system home. On the way, she removed her ball cap, glasses, and plastic teeth and wiped away the brown lipstick with a tissue.

Blanchard Avenue, with its huge Oak and Magnolia trees, had only a few streetlights, making the B and B driveway next to impossible to see in the dark. Meagan had learned exactly where the narrow turn-in to the B and B was; a few feet from a neon-yellow fire hydrant. Aunt Agnes introduced Meagan to the fire hydrant the day she arrived.

"You'll need to pick up the dog droppings around the yard and there's usually a concentration here," she said pointing to the fire hydrant.

Desperate to be accepted, Meagan nodded. She understood that poop-patrol was going to be hers. Picking up dog crap for a cheap place to live was not going to be a problem.

A single lamp burned on top of the player piano in the formal living room of the Willowby's business. Meagan crept her truck into the rear parking lot and was surprised to encounter Andrew just getting out of his car.

He waved and waited for her.

"I could use a hand moving my TV." She smiled.

Andrew looked taken aback. "That is a huge TV," he remarked. "Sure, I'll help, and you'll go to dinner with me?"

She was mildly interested in dinner with Andrew, but far more interested in moving her TV. "Okay," she agreed climbing out of the truck.

"Why are you dressed like that? Are you in the military? Where did you get this TV?" Andrew pressed.

"No, most of my clothes were stolen. This is what I had left from my husband. The TV is from a warehouse I rent." She had to lie; she had no choice.

"Oh."

Andrew helped her carry the equipment up three flights of stairs. "That took thirty minutes!" he said in surprise, as he checked his phone, again, for the time. "Hey, nice room!" Casually, he strolled around the suite, noting her lack of clothing in the closet. "Why don't you have any clothes, I mean dresses?"

"If you don't mind, I'm not a 'dress' person." She glanced at her monstrous television. "I'm a TV person."

Andrew met her eyes and murmured, "Hmm."

Six feet tall and lanky with unusually long legs, Andrew's legs looked even longer in his tight, flat, Chinos. In three steps, he was across the room and face to face with Meagan. "I'd be happy to watch TV with you. Just call me." He held a business card up and she took it. At close range, Meagan saw the pockmarked acne scars that littered his face, as well as the tip of a linear scar on his forehead. When he looked down momentarily, she noticed that the line was neat, like an incision, and snaked at least eight inches into his thick, brown hairline.

She lifted her finger to point to it. "Did you have surgery?"

"Ah, I was having headaches. Now they're gone. It was a long time ago," he replied and moved in closer. He stuck his neck out and tilted his head, preparing to kiss her. Meagan's eyes bugged out when she realized his intent. He puckered his full lips and she quickly sidestepped to the bedroom door and held it open. "I'm tired. Thanks for your help. You're pretty strong!"

Andrew set his hand on her shoulder. "I could say the same thing about you. Anytime you need help, let me know. How about I take you to dinner this weekend?"

She knew he said something, but her mind was on the pawnshop she would visit tomorrow when she resumed her hunting. Andrew squeezed her shoulder to get a response.

"Oh, okay, just text me. I'm really tired," she said leaning on the edge of the open door with her eyes closed.

"Okay, g'night."

Meagan watched Andrew stride down the hall past two guest rooms before disappearing to the left. The staircase was an echo chamber for his skillful whistling, until it faded away and she closed the door.

Her phone buzzed with a text from Rhonda, "I'm here! Are you ready?"

"Oh, my God, I forgot. Be right there!" Meagan swiftly kicked off her fatigues and slipped on old jeans and a flattering red swing top. Her overdone make-up would just have to do. She spritzed her favorite Orchid body spray here and there and dashed out the door.

Rhonda turned down the music blasting from her car stereo. "Meagan? You look fabulous! I'm glad you started wearing more makeup! Get in. Let's go have some fun!"

"I can't stay out too late. I have things to do tomorrow," Meagan confessed, trying to fluff up her flat hair.

Rhonda laughed and explained, "Yeah, yeah, yeah. Well, my mom is babysitting Alex, so I'm free and I'm ready for The Electric Panda."

Her heart wasn't completely into being social. Meagan was tired and stressing over her belongings. Rhonda was eager to meet some men, so Meagan stayed, she would be the designated driver.

Andrew pushed the window roller shade aside, enough to see Meagan sprinting to a car. "Tired? Hmm, right," he gritted and swirled the ice cubes in his Old Fashioned. Plenty of women had lied to him in his life, but they weren't his cousin. He expected a bit more courtesy from a relative. If she thought she was the only woman he was after, she was wrong. Aside from the obvious fact Meagan had model worthy looks, he could not fathom why his father was so adamant he should date Meagan; she seemed like too much effort.

Mr. Willowby made Andrew promise to pursue Meagan. "Son, a woman like that is hard to come by. You have no idea what you'd be losing," he shared. To seal the understanding, he gave his son a silver pocket watch and they shook hands.

Dismissing the thought, Andrew speed-dialed Justina and made plans for later that night. She would be more than courteous to him. Ever since he met her at The Electric Panda, Justina had been available for him whenever he called. Their sex-based relationship had been going on for three months. He knew his father wouldn't approve of his carelessness when it came to Justina. She was very private and wouldn't tell Andrew anything about her life except she enjoyed random sex and didn't have a pet in her gothically decorated apartment.

5 The Cameo

Like a precision watch, Jack's Pawn opened at the time specified on the website—ten a.m. This shop was older, Meagan presumed. Her hunch was based on the sheer amount of inventory. There was stuff everywhere! It would take years to go through everything. Suddenly she worried her family treasures could be buried somewhere in here. There was a path to follow through the store; it was a one-way and only wide enough for one person to walk at a time. A feeling of impending doom washed over her. She silently begged the god of possessions to keep hers safe.

"Can I help you?"

"Yes, Mr., ah, Lee?" she asked, noting his nametag. "I'm looking for a cameo necklace with a gold chain, a ruby rose brooch, silver pocket watch, amber ring, and an opal choker. Got any of them?"

As the small Chinese man studied the jewelry in his counter, Meagan searched also. None of her gems were there.

"Wait a minute," said Mr. Lee, digging his hand in his pocket. "Ah, yes," he confirmed as he read the note King left. "Mr. Pullman bought it, so it's at King's Pawn, maybe. You buy for a girl?"

"Yes, ah no, I am a girl," Meagan defended. Mr. Lee wore an apologetic, but bewildered look. A hot flash darkened Meagan's vision for a moment as she processed the information. She couldn't help herself, she had to know if this Mr. Pullman was the man she robbed. "Do I know him? What does he look like... the man who bought the cameo necklace?"

The manager snickered. "He's tall, spiked hair, beard, and..."

"... Mean looking?" Meagan finished. She felt her cheeks turning red at the thought that maybe he was the same man she robbed... No! Please don't be him.

Mr. Lee scowled. "Nobody ever said that about Mr. Pullman before. You go to King's Pawn and find necklace." He shooed her out of the shop, irritated someone would call King Pullman mean. He was surprised she did not have glowing words or romantic designs on the dashing King Pullman, but rather, seemed disgusted with him. That was a first.

"Thanks." She sighed .

"Sure, you go now," he urged.

In the quiet of her truck, she wondered why the man she held a gun to, who called the police on her, and then just gave her the pearls, would buy her cameo. She decided whatever his reasoning was, it was screwed up, and she intended to give him a piece of her mind. It's all she had left. She couldn't buy the cameo from him because she was flat broke, and payday wasn't for another week. He would damn well give it to her or, or, or ... There was nothing she could do about it if he didn't give it to her, but she had to try anyway.

When she arrived at King's Pawn, the five vehicles parked in front of the shop made her nervous. She worried someone might have just purchased something of hers.

King's manager, Marty, was manning the counter when Meagan stormed in, irritated. "Hi, do you have a cameo necklace for sale?"

Marty's eyes bugged out at the demanding, military garbed, biker-looking, gender-neutral person. "No. See for yourself. Sorry. Is there something else I can help you with?"

"No. Thanks."

A motley group of guys examining musical instruments in the back of the store stopped to watch her leave.

Meagan was disgusted. Since the necklace was not in the shop, it must be at Mr. Pullman's house, she concluded. So, it was back to the library where she would uncover Mr. Pullman's home address and form a fresh plan.

Agnes Willowby stood on the back porch, hands on her hips. "Young lady, why are you dressed like that and where have you been? Today is a cleaning day."

"I had errands to run and these clothes are comfortable. I'll pick up dog poop and then vacuum." Meagan tucked her t-shirt neatly into the camo pants and shook off her oversized jacket.

"Here." Ms. Willowby handed her a bucket and squeegee. "The windows need doing while you're out here." When Andrew swaggered toward them, Agnes' face brightened. "Good afternoon Andrew!"

"Hi, Mom," Andrew replied. "Well, soldier, late night, last night?" He smirked at Meagan.

When Andrew smiled, Meagan noticed something stuck in his teeth and imagined it was a piece of spinach left over from lunch. She could have gone for a big salad right about then. The exhausting search for information on Pullman kept her at the library long past the strict noon lunchtime at the B & B. Meagan ignored Andrew's goading about the fact that she went out late last night after complaining to him about how tired she was.

"Time to work!" she stated, leaving the mother and son to conspire. The quiet of her own mind was comforting as she dreamt of reclaiming her cameo, which she was positive the big man possessed.

"You'll need this," Andrew said maneuvering a sixteen-foot extension ladder to the side of the house. "I'll do the third-floor windows."

"Oh! Okay, thanks," she said surprised by his offer, but grateful. Meagan had already completed cleaning the first-floor windows across the back of the stately Victorian beauty, but she was itching to leave. With a deep sigh, she climbed the ladder to access the second-floor windows one at a time. She admitted it was kind of Andrew to willingly clean the third-floor windows for her. He knew Meagan's cleaning work covered the lion's share of her rent. Until she completed the windows on the second floor, she had to put up with his stares. His arms were crossed as he leaned against his old Pontiac, studying her. It made him seem rather creepy, Meagan thought as she focused on the windows, her aunt's cameo necklace, and her plan.

"It's all yours!" she announced, hopping off the last rungs of the tall metal ladder. Meagan handed Andrew the cleaning supplies with gusto. It was time to help in the kitchen and she was excited to learn how to prepare salmon with wild rice and whatever side dishes Mr. Willowby had dreamed up.

Meagan could be as discourteous as she wanted to him today because nothing was going to bother him. Andrew's mood was too good. Justina had made everything right for him the night before. He was a happy man.

As usual, the dinner guests were complimentary about the food and had questions about the recipe. Mr. Willowby was possessive of that information, so Meagan said very little. A lesbian couple from Louisiana and a retired couple from Indiana were thoroughly entertaining to Meagan during their meal. As the homosexual women shared the story of how they met, the retired couple stared at them in fascination. Meagan was positive that, at any moment, the elderly wife would ask the gay couple how they "did it." She didn't care to hear the answer, so she began bussing the table for Aunt Agnes. The elderly gentleman kindly pulled his curious wife away from the table with the suggestion of a stroll before dessert.

The moment the sun disappeared, Meagan set her plan in motion. It was time for her to walk the half-mile to the corner gas station to catch the cab she called earlier. She wanted no trace of her truck near the Pullman place.

She would rather have not paid for a cab, but the slimy thieves who ripped her life apart, also stole her bicycle. Several years earlier, she bought that bike because her car had died and could not be resurrected for under a thousand dollars, which she didn't have. Paxton was in Afghanistan and Meagan knew he would not be happy if she drove his truck. He was possessive that way and she refused to rock the boat by upsetting him. For twenty-five dollars, she bought a decent bike at a garage sale on her street and began riding it to work. Even after Pax died, she waited weeks before working up the nerve to drive his truck.

"Come out here," Rhonda had ordered and pulled Meagan by the arm, outside to her driveway. "I saw this and thought of you." She pointed to a sparkling bumper sticker she had affixed to the back window of Pax's truck. It read, 'Girls loves trucks too.'

"Thanks."

"Will you please stop riding that stupid bike? It's dangerous. The truck is yours now," Rhonda pleaded.

"You're right," Meagan said. "I will drive the truck." She straightened herself and apologized to Paxton in her mind, then drove that truck everywhere.

Cab fare to the crossroads near Pullman's ranch was twenty dollars, which Meagan had to scrounge for. She did a happy dance when she found an old ten-dollar bill in a pocket of Paxton's jeans. She began rooting for money in all his clothes, and discovered, to her amusement, Paxton had several hiding places. It wasn't a surprise.

"Perfect. Stop here," she said.

Wide-eyed, the cab driver looked all around the surrounding fields and warned, "Lady, it's dark and I don't think you should be walking around out here. What you gonna do if a coyote comes? I'll charge you half fare to take you back to town."

"I'm good, thanks," she said confidently, stuffing the fare and a small tip into his outstretched hand.

"Suit yourself." He rolled up his window and executed a dusty one-eighty on the gravel road.

She began the mile walk down the rural farm road. Her smartphone GPS signaled she had arrived at 107 Farm to Market road 1040, gloomy as it was. In the limited moonlight, with several lights glowing from the windows of the traditional, brick home, she knew it was the right place. Her aerial study of the layout of this property online was worth it. She had a good idea of the lay of the land and buildings. Equipped with a compass, flashlight, and the military Taser Pax kept stowed in the center compartment of his truck, she headed out to retrieve her Aunt Coral's necklace.

Meagan approached the lone, long ranch house. It had a large, half-built, second story addition sprouting up from the center of the home. She briskly sprinted across the property, making sure to stay on the grass, off to the side of the gravel and dirt driveway. The place looked lonely.

Paxton's comfortable, dark canvas camouflage pants made sneaking around easy. The dark ball cap had a connected sheet of black fabric, which covered her ears, hung down past her neck and completely concealed her light blonde hair. Paxton liked to wear it to keep the sun off his neck when he mowed the grass. The hat still smelled like him.

A horse whinnied in the distance and several far-off dogs barked. Pipe fencing surrounded acres of meadow in need of grazing or mowing. A jacked-up truck was parked next to a gold SUV, outside the detached three car garage. Meagan skirted around the massive garage to the back of the property and was surprised by the remoteness. Aside from the house, a large barn on Pullman's property was the only structure that she could see, in any direction. The property appeared to go on for miles.

Meagan squatted down behind an oversized barbeque in an outdoor cooking area. From this spot, she could see the activity inside the well-lit kitchen of Pullman's house. A woman in her thirties, wearing a t-shirt and sweat pants, seemed to be searching for something. She swung her long ponytail over her shoulder and poured two glasses of beer. A muscular man entered the room with only a towel around his waist. He raked his hands through his wet hair; he looked exhausted. Meagan's gut told her it was him—the pawn man. He looked irritated as he watched the woman for a moment before he spoke.

Meagan could see the discord; the man wanted her to leave—she wanted to have a drink with him. He won. She guzzled her beer and marched out. The broad-shouldered man rinsed out the beer bottle she left and disposed of it then whistled loudly.

When his dog rushed to his side, Meagan knew she was at the right place. That golden-faced, huge German Shepherd was one of a kind and belonged to the man she had held a gun to. She realized that bringing dog treats would have been smart. Her burning question was, "Why would that man care to own the cameo necklace?" She was positive if she could get into that house, she would find the necklace and the jewelry recovery operation would be well underway.

A light snapped on in another room on the first-floor and the man sat down on a big leather chair. He scratched an island of dark, curly hair in the center of his wide, tanned bare chest. The vertical white stripes down the sides of the sweatpants he now wore made his legs appear ten feet long. Reclining in the chair, he flipped open a laptop as the dog curled up on the western area rug at his feet.

Fortunately, the weather was moderate; conducive to outdoor spying. She tiptoed from the stoned-in kitchen to the house and stopped short beside the living room window when the shepherd growled. From this new vantage point, she could see that Pullman was intently researching information about comas.

Occasionally, Pullman would say something, causing the dog's prominent black eyebrows to move oddly. Meagan found the man and his dog, comical. She wondered who protected whom.

When the dog whined, Pullman closed his computer. He scratched and petted the shepherd then they left the room and turned off the lights. Meagan scurried back to hide in the safety of the rocked kitchen, to observe. A light in a room at the far-left end of the house caught her attention; she softly crept twenty yards to a fire pit, surrounded by numerous Adirondack chairs. The fire pit area was edged with a cluster of evergreens, which provided perfect cover while she stalked the man from the pawnshop.

"So peaceful out here," she whispered. To sit in one of those wooden chairs and stare into a blazing fire in that pit would have been heavenly. She felt pine needles stab her as she jockeyed for just the right spot to hide.

The fact that there were no blinds in the home did not escape Meagan. She was amazed someone cared so little for their privacy that they had no window coverings. In this instance, however, she was relieved. To the man inside the house, everything outside his windows was a dark blur with a coating of soft moonlight. Conversely, for Meagan, spying on this man was quickly becoming something akin to a dramatic movie and she was getting emotionally sucked in.

The room was manly and large; the walls were dark gray and adorned with taxidermized hunting trophies. Pullman picked clothing off the floor, dug in a pocket, and deposited the clothes somewhere Meagan could not see. When he propped himself against a pile of pillows on his large bed and held up the cameo necklace, Meagan's hand shot up to cover her mouth. "Why would this man give a damn about my necklace?"

The German shepherd hopped up on the vacant side of the bed and laid his huge head on Pullman's lap. The dog's eyebrows began dancing again as his big brown eyes focused on his master's face. Meagan guessed that Pullman was talking to him; probably explaining the necklace in his possession. Reaching into the drawer of his nightstand, Mr. Pullman held up the photo Meagan left behind at the pawnshop. He rubbed his temples and studied it.

"What? My photo? He's a freaking weirdo. I've got to get them back." It was disturbing, and she found it difficult to believe that he would be genuinely interested in the photo. Irritation, coupled with determination to have her family heirlooms back, fueled her plan.

She should have put more thought into the details of her mission. It was late, and she was tired; she hadn't even brought a bedroll. When Mr. Pullman fell asleep, Meagan carefully trotted back around the house to the windowless detached garage and checked the side door. She was grateful it was not locked; sleeping outside was not appealing. Despite her lack of planning, things were going well.

Exterior lighting from the house trickled into the garage when she opened the door. She could vaguely discern two vehicles and a work area designed for someone knowledgeable about cars. The flashlight she brought illuminated what should have been a third garage bay but had been transformed into a crude office with a dorm fridge and bathroom. Around the corner from the bathroom was a cot covered with a sleeping bag. “Jackpot,” Meagan said pleased. After beating the dust and cobwebs from the bedding, she slid down into the heavy-duty sleeping bag. The strong scent of Old Spice and body odor assaulted her. She focused on the cameo necklace and fell asleep, remembering the smiling faces of the people who loved her.

6 Entering

King was up before the sun. His sidekick, Storm, paced the front acreage and took care of his morning business. King's phone rang; it was Ace's phone number, but the voice on the other end was not Ace's.

"Your brother screwed me, King, and I want my money back. Twenty grand by three p.m. tomorrow, or Jack will have an accident too. Bring it to the Chester Park Amphitheatre. Use a lunch pail and be there on time. I'll be calling you again," the anonymous caller spat.

"What have you done to Ace?" King demanded.

"He's alive, if that's what you want to know."

"Storm," King said as he let the dog back in, "we've got problems." Mechanically, he called Ace's number back. No answer. Nerve-racked, King accelerated his morning routine. The safety of his parents, and Ace's condition, were all he could think about.

He shoved his legs into old jeans and tugged on a pair of his favorite cowboy boots. The supple, black leather jacket was a gift from Gayla. As much as he wished she hadn't bought it, he could not deny the comfort and fit. Accepting the gift from her meant he owed her. He suspected she worked that way. She had a good business and made a generous living as a veterinarian, but with her, everything had strings attached that kept her in his bed. The conversation about their 'arrangement' was aching to be had; it had become physically and emotionally exhausting to King. On some level, he feared her reaction and the possibility she would hurt herself.

King stood in the driveway, talking on his phone.

Meagan heard Pullman say, "Come on, Ace! Man, answer your phone!" She scrambled over to the garage door. With her face pressed up against a small crack between the garage door and the wall, Meagan watched Storm sniff the air. Pullman quit the phone call and dialed another number. "Dad, hey, where are you? Okay. I'm coming by in twenty minutes."

A small, gold SUV veered into Pullman's driveway, it was the ponytail lady Meagan remembered seeing in his kitchen. "You are persistent," Meagan mumbled.

She rushed over to Pullman and commanded, "We need to talk."

"No Gayla. I have to go." He whistled sharply, and the pointy-eared dog leaped into the truck as Pullman held the driver's side door open. "We are not talking now." Disgusted, Pullman slid onto his truck seat, ignoring Gayla as her SUV kicked up gravel and drove off in the opposite direction.

Meagan was curious about the drama she had just witnessed, but she knew first things were first; the necklace. She was pleased to discover the sink and toilet in the garage worked just fine. She washed up quickly. As she straightened the sleeping bag on the cot, the sound of gravel crunching under car tires prompted her to peer through the crack in the garage once more. It was the ponytail woman again.

In the sunlight, the strange woman appeared rougher. Her jeans were as worn as her cowboy boots. A white lab coat hung loosely over a plaid, button down shirt.

Her heavily made up eyes darted about as she scurried to Pullman's front door and used a key to get in.

"So, you are either the girlfriend or the sister. Hmm," whispered Meagan as she hustled out of the garage. She skirted around the house and ducked behind the rocks of the outdoor kitchen. The many large windows of the home offered enough light that she could see the woman was snooping for something as she poured through the kitchen drawers. Meagan lost sight of her for a few moments before she entered the living room and began searching under cushions and in cabinets.

The frustrated woman combed the entire room before she left and reappeared in Pullman's bedroom. Tentatively, she moved over to the bed, buried her head in Pullman's pillow and smelled it; then she walked around to the other side to smell the other pillow.

"What the heck!" exclaimed Meagan. "Everything to do with this guy is weird. She surely is not his sister! Pullman, your girlfriend is a fruitcake." A sharp pain stabbed at her heart. Memories from years past reminded her of a time when she stood close to Paxton, just to smell him. Suddenly, she knew—Pullman's intruder was in love with him and Meagan couldn't tear her eyes away. She felt a sudden sadness for her.

After opening every drawer and canvassing the bedroom, the woman made a phone call and departed.

When Meagan was confident the woman had left the property, she strolled around the entire house, looking for a window to breach. The windows appeared new and were unusual. They didn't move up and down, they opened like a door with a crank. To her delight, one of three windows in a spare room was open a fraction of an inch.

Back in the garage, she collected a tire iron and a bucket to stand on. "Perfect." She grinned and shoved the iron in the window gap then pushed on the crank until the opening was sufficient for her to reach in and extend the window the rest of the way. She shimmied in the window and fell on the carpeted floor.

Somewhat familiar with the room arrangement of the sparsely furnished, masculine home, Meagan marched directly to Pullman's bedroom and shuffled through the nightstand—nothing. "Rats! It must be here!"

Sitting on his tall chest of drawers was a framed photo of two handsome, clean-shaven men. She recognized one of the men as a younger version of the clerk who sold her back her guns, at Ace's Pawn. In the photo, his arm was over the taller Pullman's shoulder—the man she held up at gunpoint. There was a lake in the background, and horses. Their jeans were faded, and they wore university t-shirts and cowboy boots. Though they were squinting in the sun, they favored in their smiles, and Meagan suspected they were brothers. To be friends and relatives, that would be the ultimate gift. The photo made her smile and think of Rhonda.

"Back to business," she reminded herself.

Meagan recalled the scene where Pullman was admiring the cameo last night and concluded that it was... in his bed! She was ecstatic when she threw back the sheets and there it was. Pullman must have fallen asleep and dropped it, along with her family photo. After straightening the bed, she put the cameo on and tucked the photo in the back pocket of her jeans.

Her stomach had been growling for hours when she finally went to the kitchen. "Hmm, lots of good stuff in here." A handful of juicy grapes tasted heavenly for an appetizer. An irresistible leftover noodle dish smelled wonderful. She ate a portion of it cold, and then washed it down with a glass of milk. "Pullman, you're a good cook," she complimented, grinning and cleaning up her mess. With a belly full of food and her family necklace where it should be, Meagan was momentarily content.

Strange and exciting feelings coursed through her. Locating her heirlooms was rewarding. Her family's legacy; the jewels, the artwork, and the electronics were her mission and with every recovered item, she felt stronger. Standing in the living room, gazing out the row of new windows, Meagan could understand the draw to living remotely—it was beautiful. In the clear light of the day, she noticed a large, red barn and decent fencing in various places indicating, at one time, this was a working ranch with areas for different animals.

She strolled down a wide hallway and entered a room that faced the front acreage. "He doesn't use this room much," she mused. A clean, sizeable modern desk sat in the center of the room on a large, colorful area rug. Meagan studied the bold, thought-provoking, geometric pattern on the carpet then turned her attention to the walls. Multiple carefully framed academic awards and degrees were displayed; all belonging to Brandon K. Pullman. "Brandon?" she mumbled and melted into the comfortable leather swivel captain's chair, her hands caressing the arms. She supposed the man she robbed looked like a 'Brandon.'

The view across the driveway and gravel road was beautiful. One hundred yards ahead, cows were gathered at a fence; some black, some blonde, but all were fascinating to her. They moved gracefully along the fence line. Some stopped occasionally to poke their head through the fence and sample the grass on the other side.

If they would listen, Meagan would tell them, "The grass is the same everywhere, so don't stick your neck out." In that moment, Meagan thought about her mission and how none of her heirlooms would be coming back if she hadn't 'stuck her neck out.' "Forget I said that, cows; try it all!"

Time had evaporated since she broke into the house. She'd been dawdling in Mr. Pullman's place for over five hours when her phone vibrated in her hand, disrupting her quiet contentment. The number was unknown to her, so she let it go to her voice mail. When she checked the message moments later she discovered it was Andrew calling about dinner. She texted him, "I'm tied up; another day."

He replied, "Okay."

From her comfortable seat, she watched as a familiar SUV drove right up to the house. "Not you again," Meagan groaned. Gayla parked in Pullman's driveway, causing Meagan to scramble for somewhere to hide. Her choices were closets or under the bed. She darted across the wide hall to the master bedroom and dove to the carpeted floor under the king-size bed.

The front door opened.

Meagan could hear Gayla's resolute footsteps on the hardwood and watched her cowboy boots as she entered the bedroom.

"What do you want?" Gayla sneered into her phone as she removed her clothes. She kicked them in a pile and marched naked to the bathroom. "That's fine, I hope it works. We need it, bye," she responded and tossed the phone on the bed.

"What are you doing?" Meagan mouthed as the shower roared to life. She was one hundred percent sure ponytail woman should not be there. With nowhere to go, Meagan relaxed under the bed and waited for the spectacle to unfold. She knew she was getting caught up in Mr. Pullman's domestic issues and Rhonda would have laughed at her. But it couldn't be helped; she had to see the next episode.

7 Ace is Down

King tried to reach Ace on his phone again.

"Ha... low."

"Ace, are you okay?" King asked, agitated but relieved that Ace finally answered his phone.

"Yep...sore..."

"I'll be there in ten minutes."

"Okay..." Ace replied weakly.

With no time to dilly-dally, King made a pit-stop by Jack's Pawn and dropped off Storm to help guard Jack.

"Thank you for bringing Storm. Everyone loves him—even customers. He's a great dog," Mr. Lee admitted.

King sighed. The last thing he wanted to hear was that the customers loved his dog. "Mr. Lee, no one feeds Storm anything, except you and Jack," he reminded him.

"Oh yes, yes, Mr. King," Mr. Lee acknowledged.

King shared the news of the mysterious phone threat he received earlier. Mr. Lee was not surprised; people had threatened him bodily harm over a pawn deal before. He knew whoever was at the other end of that threating phone call would not intimidate any of the Pullman men into giving up twenty thousand dollars or tolerate a family member getting hurt.

A sense of calm came over King as he hurried to Ace's house. Mr. Lee was a funny old gentleman, who sometimes oozed wisdom; like he did today. "Everything will be fine, Mr. King. Storm good luck. You good family. You see," he had said.

King hoped he would 'see' that everything would be fine. In all the turmoil of the morning, King had forgotten to quiz Mr. Lee about his bizarre jewelry thief. He assumed that if there had been trouble at Jack's Pawn, Mr. Lee would have mentioned it. As he had previously thought, she'd probably moved on.

Everything was quiet. The front door had been left ajar. Ace's face was bloodied, and he was lying, semi-conscious, on the floor, but his house was undisturbed. King checked for a pulse at Ace's neck—it was strong. "Let's go, Ace," King ordered, helping his heavy but limp brother to the truck. "We've got to fix this."

"I'm...fine," whined Ace. "I just hurt like hell."

"She's here. Damn," King groaned. Gayla's SUV in his driveway was an unsettling sight. He half-dragged Ace; lugged him into the house and helped him to the sofa. He roused and winced in pain when King cleaned his face and addressed the cuts.

"Take this," he ordered and shoved two pills in Ace's mouth then held a water glass to his lips. "This will knock you out for a while longer. We'll talk when you wake up, Ace."

Meagan heard the pounding of boots coming toward the bedroom. Part of her wished she were anywhere else in the world except in this bedroom, under the bed. The other part of her wanted to see the show. Her heart was pounding in her ears.

"Gayla," he said sternly. "What are you doing here?"

Under the bed, Meagan rolled her eyes. "No kidding," she mouthed.

Gayla planted her hands on her hips, indignantly. "You're home early. I'm not even in bed yet," she purred. Meagan assumed Gayla was naked, though her view of the couple was limited to the knees down. As Gayla advanced toward Mr. Pullman, he backed up.

"I need some money," she confessed. "Mama's bills are high. I thought you would help me again, King."

Meagan wanted to gag. How pathetic that the woman was, selling herself out like that. She was using sex as a tool on Mr. Pullman. It occurred to her, "King?" Gayla had called him, 'King.' "King?" Meagan mouthed again as it dawned on her that she held a gun to the owner of the pawnshop. "King's Pawn, oh, no." Her quest was not going well. "Please, God, help me to not end up in jail," she prayed.

"Gayla, why are you not at work right now? You have a business to run."

Meagan blinked hard to clear her vision, but they were real. The scars on the back of the woman's right leg appeared to be tracks; suggesting she was a drug user. Thoughts of Mr. Pullman either pushing drugs or using drugs seemed absurd to Meagan. She shut her eyes, attempting to wish away the thought. No druggie she could imagine would keep his thick beard so neat or his shirts pressed to perfection. The photo on the dresser appeared in her mind. She knew virtually nothing about Mr. Pullman, but she would bet he had never done drugs.

"What are you implying?" Gayla demanded.

"I'm saying that if you paid attention to your business, you wouldn't need to be asking me for money. I have enough issues with my own family right now. I'm sorry, but I can't help you," he said regretfully but firmly.

Gayla was on a roll. "We're family. Just sell something for Christ's sake! Aren't I worth it?" she shouted, slapping his arm, hard and launching herself onto the bed.

"I'm not leaving, King. I need you right here beside me," she declared.

King didn't budge. "You need to go," he said and quickly left the room.

"You're making a mistake," Gayla shouted and stomped to the bathroom. A few moments later, she emerged, dressed. She slid open the ceiling-height, mirrored closet door. Meagan couldn't see what the woman was doing, but she dropped a large, glistening ring on the carpet and quickly picked it up. She slid the door shut and exited the room.

"How screwed up is this guy's life?" Meagan mused. "He works at a pawn shop, or rather, owns a pawn shop, and comes home to this trash?" She couldn't fathom ever yelling at Paxton like that. Suddenly her emotionally empty, roller coaster, ten-year life with Paxton didn't seem so bad; at least he didn't spend all their money on drugs. Sure, he had his anger issues, but, as Meagan learned years ago, keeping the peace meant keeping her mouth shut and agreeing with Paxton.

The regular boxing matches Paxton insisted on having with her were for her benefit, he claimed. Truth be told, they did help her. The day she inadvertently clocked Paxton with a perfect right hook and sent him to the mat, something changed in her; she tasted power for the first time. Paxton changed too; he became more and more emotionally closed off until his unit was called back to Afghanistan where his life was taken.

Chasing after King, Gayla hurried through the living room and stopped near the injured, sleeping man on the sofa. Meagan heard her say loudly, "You weren't kidding about having family problems. Good luck. Call me if you want some action. You know I love you."

The front door slammed shut.

Someone was cooking, and the scent was dreamy. Meagan considered bolting out of Pullman's bedroom and hiding somewhere, anywhere else, until she heard his boots on the hardwood floor. Mr. Pullman headed back to his bedroom, talking on the phone. "Dad," he warned, "I want you to be careful. Ace has some guy pissed off and he is threatening our family."

On speakerphone, Meagan listened to the man's response. "What the hell! Do you have the details?"

"No. But I will get answers when Ace comes to," King promised. "Any sign of that son of a bitch in military garb?"

A cold chill ran down Meagan's spine. She considered herself a good judge of character, but she may have misjudged Mr. Pullman. Suddenly, he seemed bigger, tougher, and more than capable of destroying her.

"I haven't seen him. I'll let you know if he comes in my shop. Later, son."

"Thanks, Dad, I don't want any shots fired."

Meagan did not realize she inadvertently made herself the target of revengeful pawnshop owners all over town. Perspiring profusely and confined under the bed, she thought she might pass out. This must be what it felt like to have your face plastered on a 'wanted' poster in the post office. She'd take that over having her face plastered on a milk carton, however. Milk carton photos meant that she was probably dead, whereas the 'wanted' poster advertised someone alive and on the run. She was okay with that.

A timer buzzed in the kitchen and Pullman left the bedroom. Meagan shimmied out from under the bed and ran to the impeccable master bathroom to relieve herself. No flushing, as it could have attracted attention. Undoubtedly this was the cleanest bathroom Meagan had ever used—everything was white—all the tile and towels. Her fingers feathered the length of the cool, white granite counter top infused with subtle streaks of gray.

Tired of lying on her stomach under the bed, she nestled herself in between the heavy men's clothes and suitcases in the expansive closet behind the sliding doors.

When she was safely ensconced, a sliver of light reflected off metal near her; she discovered a built-in gun compartment nearby. Blindly feeling around, she found another flashlight, only this heavy-duty, amazing tool had multiple light settings. She flicked it on to examine the rifles closely. Her knowledge of guns was limited to handguns, but these firearms were beautiful nonetheless. Meagan opened a compact, heavy box, like the one she was sitting on. It was full of books. There had to be hundreds; some paperbacks, some hardcover. She smothered the laugh that tried to escape as she read the book titles; Only You, Sleeping with the Prince, A Lady for the Duke, and Spice Up Your Marriage in Three Steps. Maybe these books belonged to Gayla the slapper? Regardless, she needed a way to pass the time, so she selected, 'A Lady for the Duke', and read by flashlight.

From his spot at the kitchen bar where King sat eating his dinner, he kept an eye on Ace and romanced about the hundreds of acres he longed to work cattle on. He tried not to think about the existence of people who purposefully wanted to hurt his family. It burned him.

After washing his dinner dishes, he surveyed his pitiful progress on the room addition and checked on his mom.

"Hi Mom!" he spoke into his phone as he whipped into the master bathroom. Meagan shut off her light. "I can't believe you answered the phone!" King was elated his mother had woken up.

"I'll see you shortly," he said before ending the call.

King felt an urgency to check on his parents. Ace was still out cold, so he left a note for him on the living room end table.

Meagan surmised Mr. Pullman was happy about something involving his mother and was anxious to leave. In minutes, his truck kicked up gravel as he departed for the hospital.

8 Shooter

The tall door slid open smoothly. Meagan fumbled out of the closet, sprinted down the hall, and stopped curiously at a bedroom. The door must have been closed earlier or she would have noticed the child's room. Nothing about Mr. Pullman indicated he might be a father; the room seemed absurd in his house. The walls were pink and green. A twin sleigh bed was parked next to an antique baby crib full of stuffed animals clustered together around a pink chenille pillow. An old, white rocking chair graced the center of a pale green rag rug; a child's book had been left on the seat.

A loud cracking sound sent adrenaline coursing through her. She darted several doors down the hall to the office with the view of the cows. She hid around the corner and listened to a strange male voice.

"Shit! Ow!" he complained. He was rattling pans about in the kitchen. Her hand automatically groped for the comfort of the gun in her pocket.

"What on earth?" she muttered when car headlights flashed through the room, then abruptly shut off. A vehicle was in Mr. Pullman's driveway, twenty feet from the office where Meagan stood. Two men got out quickly. Before they reached the front door, Meagan ran to hide behind the leather couch in the living room; from there she could see them enter. Her hands were shaking.

The men shot the locks and kicked in the front door. They barged in wearing ski masks and pointed their guns at someone in the kitchen out of Meagan's line of sight. One assailant was short and the other fat. She steadied her gun on the sofa, took aim, and shot the fat man in the back. His knees buckled, and he fell like a building. His gun slid across the shiny oak floor. "What the hell?" the short intruder in the kitchen shouted to Ace, "You're here?"

"What the ...?" whipped around to face them; he had had had enough of those bozos. When the short trespasser looked toward his injured buddy, Ace whacked the gun out of his hand with a skillet. The masked man hurled a punch to Ace's face, knocking him to the kitchen floor.

Meagan had to get out of Pullman's house. She bolted through the living room and fired her gun at the man who was pummeling Ace; striking him once in the back of each leg. She flew out the busted front door to the garage side entry. Meagan wondered who they were after. She got a glimpse of the bloodied man on the floor in the kitchen and it wasn't Mr. Pullman; she didn't know who it was. The short man was wailing and begging 911 to hurry while Meagan lurked in the garage to see what would happen next.

"I refuse to die here," the short man screamed. "Arty? Art?" he cried, but his friend was not conscious. "Please don't die, buddy."

Sticking around Mr. Pullman's place when there could be a double or triple homicide in his house was foolish. Maybe she should have run to the crossroads and called a cab. Another set of car lights kept Meagan from hauling ass down the main road. Instead, she stayed hidden inside the garage and watched matters unfold through the crack in the door. She witnessed an elderly, bearded man in a plaid jacket hop out of his Hummer. "No! No!" he mumbled worriedly at the sight of the front door damage then hurried into the house.

The police arrived at the same time as the ambulance; Meagan was relieved to see them haul off the two masked men that she shot. Thank goodness, they were still alive, but what about the man in the kitchen? She had yet to see him.

"Someone shot me! They're still in there!" screamed the criminal with a bullet in each leg. The medics strapped him to the gurney. "You should be looking for them," he continued, pleading with the officers.

The older man, Officer Rhodes, responded, "We will. It's just more difficult when we have no idea what they look like." He rolled his eyes at the other officer who shrugged and visually canvassed the Pullman property. "They likely didn't get too far," he continued. "Officer Gage will look around."

Both policemen were curious, but neither was gnawing at the bit to apprehend the mystery shooter of the two men who broke into Pullman's place. As the injured men were loaded into the ambulance, Officer Rhodes asked, "You were injured as you were committing a crime. Tell me why we should hurry to find the shooter?"

The injured man groaned, his misery compounded by the phantom, unexpected gunman.

Meagan saw the old man emerge from the house. He was assisting the bloody-faced, younger man; the apparent target of the break-in.

Officer Gage approached them and asked, "Who shot these men?"

Ace answered, "I wish I knew. I'd like to thank them. I didn't see anyone."

"Damnedest thing," the old man injected.

Gage pressed Ace, "Why were these men after you?"

Ace shrugged his shoulders. "Seems like one of them thinks I owe them money. I don't. I don't owe anybody money."

Jack Pullman studied his son's face then told the officer, "Let us know if you need anything else from us."

"Will do. Mind if we search the house first?"

Jack and Ace stepped aside for the men.

It occurred to Ace if Jack had arrived a few seconds earlier, he could have been shot. "Dad, why are you here?"

Meagan sucked in a breath when the old man took a ruby brooch out of his pocket to show his son. The porch light was enough for Meagan to clearly see what Jack held. "I stopped by to bring him this. King asked me to give this to him, if it found its way to my shop; said he thought your mother might like something like it."

Ace examined it. "Hmm, that's strange. I didn't know he cared about shit like this."

"Me too," Jack agreed, re-pocketing the piece. "Oh, well."

The officers wrapped up their search of the house and made a beeline for the garage. Meagan locked the door to stall them. She then climbed in the trunk of a sixty-seven Mustang and pulled the lid shut.

"You gonna let us in the garage, Jack?" Officer Rhodes called. "It's locked."

"Sure," Jack replied fidgeting for the right key. "Here you go." He turned the lights on in the garage as the men searched for clues. Jack was happy to answer questions about the cars he had been restoring for years and promised the officers they could take the Mustang out when the restoration was complete.

When their brief evaluation of the garage produced no criminal element, the police left. Jack disappeared into the house to deposit the brooch, and then reappeared in the driveway. He informed his youngest son, "Ace, you're coming with me. We're going to the hospital to get your face looked at and check on your mother."

Shining her flashlight, Meagan located and popped the trunk release and climbed out. She was rested, but hungry again. Through the crack in the wall, she checked, and the driveway was finally empty.

"Hmm," she mumbled pensively. Even though the lock was busted, the heavy, wooden front door still closed. "Shame on them," Meagan whispered, staring at the disaster they left for Pullman. "He doesn't deserve this."

Meagan inhaled deeply and began sweeping and wiping blood and food off the floor with wet paper towels until the kitchen looked decent again. She briefly removed her thin leather gloves to wash her hands and raid Pullman's fridge. This time she finished the amazing cold noodle casserole. She couldn't help but wonder what the old man did with the ruby brooch he brought home for Mr. Pullman. It's got to be right around here. Tummy full of food and too tired from the day's stress to search tonight, she trudged to Pullman's bedroom and crawled back under the bed; content and exhilarated. She was right where she needed to be. Her heart warmed knowing there was another precious jewel of hers in the house.

9 Livestock

King was visiting his mother at the hospital when Jack called. "Son, your house was broken into and two men went after Ace. I think they thought he was you."

"Again? Is he, alright? Who were they?"

"Yes, he's going to be okay. Damnedest thing, someone shot the men and saved Ace. He didn't know either of the intruders, but he thinks they were the same guys who broke into his house."

King was dumbfounded. "Why? What do they want?"

"That's the thing. They claim he owes them money. I'm taking Ace to the hospital to get checked out. Storm is still at my shop."

"Yeah, okay, thanks, Dad."

King shared the news with his mother before leaving the hospital. Her recovery was remarkable. With his family dodging bullets from every direction lately, his mother's health was great news.

A livestock delivery was scheduled to arrive at the ranch early in the morning and King needed his wits about him. After a reassuring visit, he kissed his mother on the cheek and headed home to sleep.

Except for the lockset, the front door could be salvaged, which was a relief since it was an expensive, special order, solid core door. King's jaw dropped when he entered his kitchen. He could not fit his father's version of the break-in with the immaculate condition of his home. In fact, if it weren't for the front door, he would have thought his dad had made up the entire story. "Hmm, people were shot in here? Huh."

Until he could make time to fix the door properly, he screwed the door to the jamb.

He popped open a cold beer, removed his boots, and rummaged through his fridge; stomach growling. Ace must have eaten the noodle casserole, the empty container was rinsed and sitting in the sink. He decided to cook a frittata, so he whipped half a dozen eggs together, added chopped mushrooms and peppers, and a few crumbles of cooked turkey sausage. While the frittata baked, King headed back to the bedroom. His house seemed barren without Storm.

He stripped and tossed his clothes in the bedroom hamper at the far end of the room. With plenty of time to shower, he dropped naked to the carpet for one hundred pushups. He had always been a strong man; spot exercising, sometimes half a dozen times in a day, kept him on point, physically.

"Ninety-nine, one hundred," he gritted, resting on the carpet for a moment. A small snoring sound caught his attention and he glanced over at the bed. He blinked repeatedly to ensure his vision was not failing him. From his prone position on the floor, he stared, in shock, at the form under his bed. The face was turned away and a black head-cover concealed the hair, but he was certain it was the same person who robbed him at gunpoint. Long legs, those black boots, and the camo pants were a dead giveaway.

"Holy crap," he whispered. Endorphins coursing through his veins forced him to resume his pushups. "It was her, or him, who must have shot those guys and saved Ace... and probably cleaned up the mess." He zeroed in on the delicate wrist and hand with long tapered fingers; the hand of a woman. A warm feeling of being protected engulfed him. "What the heck is she doing...?" His mind raced to the necklace... and the photo. With a big sigh, King fell flat once more for a good look then refocused and hopped in the shower. "Unbelievable."

He ate three slices of his frittata and the remaining three slices would make great leftovers—if Robber Girl didn't raid his fridge. The myriad of things King should have been thinking about took a backseat as he contemplated the pearls and the other gems he remembered seeing in the photo. He smirked and shook his head pondering his under-the-bed intruder. "Ah, hell, she can deal with the results of her own actions." He decided to ignore her because although he gave her the pearls, she saved Ace's life. Technically, he owed her. After checking his email, he grabbed his handy Ruger pistol from its safe spot in his office and slipped into bed, amazed at the day's turn of events. It was a strange turn of events. As worried as he had been about the robber confronting Jack; instead, she was under his bed, with a loaded pistol, snoring.

When his alarm blared at five a.m., King shuffled to the bathroom, stripping off his jockey shorts. He recalled his intruder, who, at that moment, must have had a great view of his ass.

Only, she didn't, because she wasn't there. In the middle of the night, she snuck out of the house through the mudroom and walked down to the barn; her curiosity piqued. A door on the north side of the barn, not visible from the house, opened easily for her. Never had she encountered so many unlocked doors. "Must be how life is, in the country."

She was in an office; another hyper-clean room, only it was in a barn! A rectangular rug depicting a gathering of horses at a river, covered the smooth concrete floor. Scads of photos of Mr. Pullman and his brother on horseback or fishing blanketed the walls. She patrolled a tack room that lead to horse stalls, then returned to the organized office. Meagan suspected the sterile barn had not housed horses in a long time. Mr. Pullman's superior flashlight was the perfect tool for her outing. Relaxing in the swivel desk chair, she scooted closer to the desk and turned on the computer. Closing her eyes, she knew that whatever else might happen, she was going to remember this amazing place; Mr. Pullman's interesting house with all its character... and the barn. Why she had previously thought a barn had to be disgusting, she did not know; this one oozed charm and love.

The monitor glowed and she began to search Drakeslist. She perused hundreds of artwork postings and there it was; her painting. Her eyes misted with pleasure. She was elated to find the gorgeous G. Harvey painting bestowed to her by her Aunt Opal. The artist's use of light sparkling off the cowboys and their horses in the early morning rain was eerily beautiful. "I'll get you back. Don't worry," she promised, tapping the screen with a pen. In a quick text to the seller, she requested a meeting time for the next day at nine p.m. A vehicle approaching the barn caught Meagan off guard. Frantically, she clicked out of Drakeslist and hurried up the ladder to the loft, to avoid being seen.

The twelve-foot tall double barn doors opened simultaneously, and Pullman yelled, "Back her up!"

Meagan stifled a snicker when the truck driver grabbed the leads of four alpacas and a donkey and ushered the agitated bunch out of the trailer. She imagined horses—

fine quarter horses—on this land, not half a dozen one hundred and fifty-pound, long-legged, ugly sheep and a jackass! "What curious animals," she mumbled; she had never seen anything like them. Their camel-looking faces and big lips struck her as comical atop a long neck attached to a sheep's body, but with long legs. The donkey was normal, in her estimation.

"They need to graze in a fenced area," the driver stated. "They can run at a pretty good clip. You don't want to chase 'em."

"Got it," Pullman assured and saluted the deliveryman as he drove away. With the alpacas' leashes in one hand and the donkey's in the other, he guided them to a fenced field with a lean-to, fifty feet from the barn.

From high in the loft where Meagan hid, ignoring the poking straw, she had a great view out the massive barn doors. The rising sun twinkled off the dew on the meadow, doubling its brilliance. She checked the time on her phone and realized she had already been up for five hours.

Several of the wooly creatures made loud, humming sounds. Meagan choked back tears of laughter when Pullman got a swift kick in the calf by one of his new flock on their way to the east acreage.

She took the opportunity to scramble back to the house, through the mudroom, down the dark hall, and into Pullman's bedroom. Her phone alerted her to a text. The sellers of the G. Harvey agreed to a nine-p.m. meeting in the parking lot of a closed accounting firm.

Pullman spent hours tending to his flock. Meagan sat on his bed; she could watch this new rancher all day if she could stop the intense fatigue overtaking her. Pullman walking into the barn office was her opportunity to leave the house. She made a run for the garage. The smelly old cot was a welcome sight.

She was awakened from her nap by the sound of hammering. The crack in the wall allowed her to see him, shirtless, on his roof, working on an addition. She was intrigued when he stopped hammering to eat lunch up there.

"No! Shit!" he yelled, standing up on the roof. "Come back!"

Meagan had no clue what he was yelling about until the object of Pullman's distress galloped past the garage. Apparently, alpacas liked to run free. King shed his tool belt and hopped off his roof like a monkey, to chase the fluffy creature. Based on the distant sound of his voice, Meagan calculated that Pullman was far enough away that she could sneak back into his house.

She estimated Pullman was several miles down the road trying to capture his wayward beast, which gave her time to hunt. Not a cabinet or drawer in Pullman's bedroom and master bathroom escaped her. A glance at the time on her phone and she was disgusted with her lack of progress. She fully expected to have found her brooch by now. Tomorrow, she would search again.

In the evening, confined in his closet, she glimpsed him talking on his phone as he shed his clothes and dumped them in the hamper. He casually glanced back to the heavy, sliding door mirror, looking for her reflection under the bed. She wasn't there. Knowing she could be anywhere in his house, he refused to be rattled by her game and proceeded to take a fast shower.

Naked, he ruffled a thick towel through his very short, chestnut hair. A feeling of eyes on his skin irked him and he quickly pulled boxer shorts from his dresser. He would bet an alpaca that she was in the closet. She surely hadn't eaten in a while. Out of kindness, he left the sliding door to the closet open and climbed in bed, exhausted. His legs hadn't felt this drained since he ran track in the tenth grade.

Meagan racked her brain for a plan that did not include shooting this man for her brooch. When he left the house in the morning, for work, she would dig for it. She wanted the brooch before she met with the sellers of the painting, so she wouldn't have to return to Pullman's house. Perched on a stack of sweaters on top of a book box in the corner of Pullman's closet, Meagan returned to the story of A Lady for the Duke, until she finally dozed off.

A heavenly smell nudged her awake. It was five a.m. "This guy is nuts," she gritted.

Pullman ambled into the bathroom to brush his teeth. Something about being watched by the mesmerizing woman who robbed him and saved his brother made his skin tingle. His phone rang; it was Ace. Meagan heard Pullman say, "Sure, that's a good idea, see you later. We'll look around." For the first time, he smiled as he glanced across the room to the mirror. Meagan felt naked and exposed though she couldn't be visible to him. She hadn't thought about Pullman in any way, other than, 'the slightly scary pawnshop man who didn't turn her over to the police.' But, with that handsome, happy face peering in her direction, other adjectives came to mind; like strapping, provocative, and complex. Descriptive words she had never used for a man, surfaced. No man had ever made her sweat with his smile, until then. For a split second, she wished he would catch her in his closet.

When King left the house, Meagan ran to the kitchen. She shoved fruit, some frittata, and pancakes into a bag then noticed the front door was open and the lockset was new and that his truck was still in the driveway. A quick glance out the kitchen windows assured her he was tending his flock for the time being. He hadn't left for work. How would she ever get anything done if he was going to hang around all day? Irritated, but grateful for the food, she scampered to the garage to eat in peace and think.

Mr. Pullman's frittata put Mr. Willowby's efforts to shame and that was saying a lot. Mr. Willowby had cooked his entire life. Stuffed, she snuggled into the sleeping bag on the cot and napped hard until crunching gravel and a plethora of voices woke her, hours later.

Peering through the crack, Meagan saw Pullman greet the same two men from yesterday. She recognized the elderly man with the brooch for King, and the man she saved, who ironically enough, was also the man she bought her guns back from. The puzzle was coming together; this was Mr. Pullman's family; father, and bloody faced brother. The German shepherd happily trotted around sniffing while King helped a feeble woman out of the visiting couple's camouflage Hummer. Meagan was certain she was his mother. "I guess he's having a dinner party. I know the food will be good!" She chuckled.

"I'd like to see your new livestock, son," his father said, and Meagan snickered again at the memory in the barn. It occurred to her that even though her situation was dire, she hadn't been this amused in a long time.

Her phone buzzed with a text from Andrew. "Where are you? Mom is worried."

She responded, "Out of town. Back later." The mention of Aunt Agnes brought the B & B to mind; she could use a hot bath in the claw foot tub.

Ace escorted his mother into the house while the gray-haired man and King headed to the garage. Meagan straightened the cot and nervously hid behind the bathroom door.

"I wanted to talk to you privately," said Jack.

"I'm glad you brought Mom here. Is everything okay?"

"I think she'll heal faster here, son. As easy as that new garden home of ours is to keep up, your mother doesn't stop working. Thanks for having us. After the robberies and break-ins, she said she feels safest with you."

"I don't know about that," King lamented. "Whatever helps her, Dad."

"King, I'm going to hire some help." Jack shared. "I need someone to care for your Mom while she needs it... and the house; make it easier on everyone. I'll advertise in the town paper for someone close by."

King imagined Gayla would pitch a fit if she thought he was spending money on a caretaker-housekeeper, when he said he had none to give her. King agreed, "Sounds fine."

"We don't want to be a burden," added Jack; emotion thickened his tone.

"You're not, Dad."

Jack wiped a hand over his face. "Are you enjoying the ranch?"

"I am. It's great."

"Yeah, it is. It is."

King patted his father on the shoulder. They discussed the work left to be done on the Mustang before they left the garage. The lock on the side door clicked and Meagan finally breathed. Anxiously, she called for a cab to meet her at eight thirty at the crossroads. Her fingers touched the cameo pendant around her neck; a pleasant reminder that she had accomplished what she came to the ranch for. But things had changed, evolved, and now she knew the ruby brooch was in that house. The luminescent G. Harvey painting awaited its rightful owner and she would be there soon; then she would return to Pullman's and get her brooch back.

10 The Painting

In the rural darkness of the crossroads, half a mile from King Pullman's house, Meagan slipped into the back seat of the yellow cab and ordered, "Arndell Accounting on Center Ave."

Night time out in the country was black. A few stars littered the sky with a sliver of a moon for company. She thought about her current job and the raises she had turned down over the years. The position Pullman's father was going to advertise would be a convenient way of getting her brooch ... and a nice place to work—with that heavenly food and all. A shiver rippled through her body as she imagined the handsome man; she chalked it up to nerves.

"This place is closed, lady," the cabbie warned.

"I'm meeting some people and I need you to stay here for three minutes and wait for me. Please?"

"Ah, okay. Meter's running."

In the dim light of street lamps, Meagan marched across the parking lot to meet a heavyset lady in her thirties. The woman slurped her coke. "You here for the painting?" she asked looking Meagan up and down.

"Yes."

The seller nervously swayed from foot to foot. "Are you in the military?" she asked; her beady eyes studied Meagan's large black boots.

"No."

Meagan approached the woman's open trunk where the artwork was displayed. She scanned the painting carefully with her flashlight.

"You must know art?" the seller commented.

"Sort of," Meagan admitted and tilted the painting to see her family name on the back. "I know when it's stolen." She lifted the painting out of the trunk and pointed her gun at the woman. "You better get lost fast, because I don't feel merciful."

The woman threw her hands in the air yelling, "Oh my god! Damn it, I didn't know! My brother gave it to me. Shit!" She awkwardly clambered into her car and squealed out of the parking lot with her window down, shouting, "You're insane!"

"We can go now," Meagan told the cabbie. The painting barely fit in the back seat.

"Nice painting!" exclaimed the driver. "Why did that woman run from you?"

"Thanks. It's an heirloom. She developed a sudden case of diarrhea."

"Oh, bummer."

The B & B was dead quiet with only one car in the rear parking lot, when the yellow cab dropped Meagan off. With any luck, Andrew wouldn't be home.

"I was wondering when I would see you again," said a voice in the dark.

Clearly, her luck had run out. "Is that you, Andrew?"

"Yes. Where have you been? You weren't at work," he informed her, disgusted.

She spilled the thoughts that had been consuming her mind for the last half hour. "I was off today. I'm thinking about changing jobs. Where is your car?"

Andrew smirked. "Have you been 'late night shopping' again? Art work now, hmm."

"I have a warehouse unit and I'm decorating my room! Remember?" As far as Meagan was concerned, their conversation was over. She marched adamantly up the steps past her interrogator. "Good night, Andrew."

"Ah, did you ask Mom about that?"

She froze on the top step. "About decorating? Not yet. I plan to," she fibbed. Asking Aunt Agnes about putting her stuff in her room didn't even occur to her. What business was it of hers anyway; Meagan earned that room each day. Andrew was beginning to feel like a thorn in her side.

"Yeah, you probably should ... ask her." There was a smile in his voice that drove the thorn in further. "How about dinner Friday night at Angelo's?" he asked with a newfound confidence. "We are cousins, after all."

He was correct about the fact that they were related. Although he was annoying at times, if he could manipulate his mother in favor of the stuff Meagan wanted to keep in her room ... "6:00?"

"Ah, sure."

She could tell he was still smiling, but what the heck. One dinner with a very distant relative couldn't hurt, and since she wasn't swimming in relatives, she would go. Somberly, she added, "I'll meet you there."

"Awesome, want me to carry your pain ..."

"No. I've got it!" she insisted.

Moments later, she was in the comfort of her quaint bedroom. She laid the painting on the bed and sat down next to it. If the cozy, antique room told its secrets, Meagan was positive there would have been lovers; split apart by a war. She could imagine the woman standing at the tall, slim window, staring through the hand-made delicate curtains, out towards a distant ocean. A man like Pullman would have offered to light a fire for her because she looked chilled and afraid to be alone. But, Meagan knew the woman at the window was not chilled. She was frozen to the bone because of her loss. She couldn't cry because tears were useless, they would not bring her lover back.

There was no 'woman at the window.' The muscles in Meagan's jaw flexed involuntarily with anger over the war that separated the lovers. The imaginary scene left her heartsick for her parents, who were taken away by a plane crash. If her speed bag were mounted in the room, she would have punched it for an hour, like she used to, before it was stolen.

The unusual sound of a revving motor in the parking lot drew Meagan to her window. Towering oak trees limited her view, but she recognized Mr. Willowby. It appeared he bought a new car. As far as Meagan knew, the couple had shared a vehicle, until then. She snickered at his choice of cars; a Corvette convertible. The fact that he could fit behind the wheel of that car was impressive, as Mr. Willowby's bulbous abdomen would surely press against the steering wheel. Andrew appeared in the parking lot to meet Mr. Willowby. "Hmm, what are you up to, Andrew?" Meagan mumbled realizing she was observing a transaction.

"It's fast," Mr. Willowby warned.

Andrew grinned. "Perfect!" Then he got in the Corvette and drove away.

"Strange." Meagan would never have pegged Andrew as a Corvette person. For some reason, her thoughts put Andrew behind the wheel of a Volvo sedan, or a Saab; they're unusual, well groomed, and snobbish. Maybe the car Andrew was driving belonged to Mr. Willowby, which made sense, it was a plain old Pontiac; so much for the intriguing Mr. Willowby. The unreserved, sporty Corvette belonged to Andrew. Where he went in that car at that hour was not an issue worthy of Meagan's time. She dismissed his bizarre behavior with a wave of her hand.

Glancing down at her recovered painting, Meagan's mood picked up; another one of her soldiers was home. She wrapped the large, gold-framed canvas in a blanket and set it in the closet, praying Agnes would not find it. She was sure her aunt would be getting on her case tomorrow because the plumbing rattled whenever she bathed, and it disturbed the other guests. Meagan knew it was late, but she didn't care right then. She craved the steaming, hot water hitting her skin as she planned the recovery of her ruby brooch and the opal velvet choker.

It was comforting to have his parents and his brother home at the ranch. Apart from a few years in a dorm and his own apartment, the ranch was the only home King had known.

Jack Pullman had insisted they grill steaks outside to celebrate Brenda's hospital release. Standing around the grill, drinking a beer and talking politics, the three men reminisced.

From her seat at the kitchen table, Brenda watched the flames from the grill light up the faces of the three men she loved. She loved being Jack's wife and mother to King and Ace. More than anything, those three men mattered most.

They enjoyed spectacular bacon wrapped filet mignon, twice baked potatoes, and a tossed green salad. King put decaf coffee on to brew and began to clear the table. "Mom, go sit down with Dad in the living room, Ace and I can handle the dishes."

"Dude," Ace whined, "I'm hurt, remember? I'm gonna lay on the couch too."

King didn't mind taking care of the after-dinner dishes; he found it cathartic. He scooped leftovers into a plastic container and smiled at the thought of Storm's face when Jack would have the pleasure of surprising him with steak and potatoes.

Was she watching him right now? King wondered how his pearl thief was getting along; it had been a while since he noticed food missing. He had wrapped his brain around the fact that she could be anywhere in or around his house, but her charade was beginning to wear on him. What was the worst thing that could happen if he rousted her out and made her talk? There was no way he would let her get away like he did at the shop. Little did anyone know that King was an accomplished marksman; adept with pistols and rifles. He was ready to end her game.

"Kitchen is clean, I'm going to shower." He marched past his half-asleep family in the living room, on his way to boot the criminal out of his house.

His heart was pounding as he tucked his pistol in the waistband of his jeans, but it had to be done. Robber Girl, whoever she was, would not hide in his house any longer while his family was there—that was simply not going to happen.

He flung the tall, mirrored closet door open and rifled through the contents; shoving clothes aside and pushing boxes out of the way until it was clear she wasn't there. "You shoot like a man, but apparently, you enjoy Mom's romance novels," he stated through clenched teeth. Arms crossed over his chest, he scowled. "You will not win." He swiftly dropped to the floor beside the bed, fully expecting her to be there.

"Where in the hell are you?"

There was nothing he could do unless he chose to involve the police. Any way King sliced it, he would have looked like a fool for giving her the pearls and not turning her over to Dell. Lately he felt his 'gut feeling' had been failing him, but he believed that since she had her cameo and probably the photo, she would not be back. "Trust your gut," Jack always told him.

So, he did.

11 The Interview

Searching through the Danville News, online, Meagan re-read the ad, “Caretaker wanted; must be a hard-worker, honest, and kind. Light housekeeping and personal helper.”

She stared at her phone and began to perspire, though she couldn’t pinpoint exactly why. Setting her McDonald’s coffee down beside the library computer, she dialed the number in the ad and asked for Jack.

“Jack here,” he answered.

Hi,” Megan said nervously hoping she wasn’t being over-heard. “I’m calling about the ad in the paper for a caretaker?”

“Ah!” Jack said. He had not thought a response to his ad would happen so quickly, but he was not going to kick a gift horse in the mouth. “What are your qualifications?”

She had picked up her pen and was absent-mindedly sketching pictures of her heirlooms on a scratch pad. “I’m honest and hardworking, and I can start right away,” Meagan replied confidently.

“Fine. Meet me at 107 Farm to Market road 1040, at three today for an interview,” he instructed.

“Wonderful, thank you,” she responded. “I’ll be there.”

Meagan had only worked in an appliance office and worn jeans, so the "caretaker" position she was pursuing was quite different. On the Internet, she searched for information regarding appropriate clothing for her interview and learned that what few clothes she had were not suitable.

A text came in from Rhonda, "Hi, how about karaoke tonight?"

"I can't," Meagan explained, "I have a job interview. Help! What should I wear?"

Is your interviewer a man or a woman?" Rhonda asked.

"A man."

"Wear a short skirt and tight sweater...and heels...and wear your hair down and fluffy. You'll get the job. How about karaoke Tuesday, then? I want to hear about your job!"

Meagan saw the logic regarding the tight clothes, but it seemed like cheating. "Ah, Tuesday sounds fine. I'll meet you at The Electric Panda at nine?"

Rhonda sucked in a deep breath. "The karaoke starts at eight. Be there before eight. Please!"

"Okay. I don't see the difference an hour will make, but, okay," Meagan conceded. "I've got to go. I'll tell you all about the job, then."

Meagan had never interviewed for a job, ever. The appliance store took her application, showed her the desk she would be working at, and told her to start at nine the next morning. That was twelve years ago.

Everything surrounding the Caretaker job was different because her heirloom family was still out there, and the ruby rose was in King's house. She paced her bedroom, thinking about possible questions Jack might ask and possible answers she might give. The process was making her more anxious, not to mention the shoes she chose for the occasion. She regretted sending Rhonda a picture of the high heels from the store because Rhonda's return text was, "Yes! Buy them!"

Meagan's nerves were causing her hands to shake, but not her resolve. She parked in the driveway next to King Pullman's truck, and tried not to fall as her heels skidded off the driveway rocks. She tugged her black skirt down a bit, already remorseful about buying the shorter of two skirts. The hot rollers and hair spray worked; her head felt huge with fluffy curls cascading to the middle of her back. Her credit card needed this job desperately. She spent more on the pink angora sweater she was wearing, than she did on her first car. It was money she didn't have. She rang the doorbell.

"Just a second," King shouted.

A fabulous aroma suggested he was cooking again. She breathed it in and it made her hungry.

"Oh, hi," he said, perplexed.

"Hi, I'm here about the job? I talked to Jack."

"Oh sure, come on in. Have a seat." King rushed to the kitchen to remove something from the oven.

"Who is it, dear?" Mrs. Pullman asked.

"Mom, this is..." King began.

"Hello, I'm Meagan Cal ... Morris. I'm here about..."

"...The housekeeping job," he finished to his mother. "I need the help." He smiled warmly.

Brenda's face registered shock. "Do you mean, she's a m-maid?" she slurred a bit and pointed at Meagan with her cane.

Sensing the awkwardness, Megan responded, "Yes, I like to clean and help with anything, in general."

A quick stern look at her red-faced son, and Brenda shook her head in disbelief. "You g-go ahead with the interview s-son, don't mind me. That's a beautiful sa ... sweater," declared Mrs. Pullman.

Meagan lowered her eyes. "Thank you."

King sat in the club chair across from the sofa, where the soft, pink sweater was. There was no escaping the fact that his potential employee was beautiful. Her full, pale pink, glossy lips moved, but King was having difficulty hearing.

Mrs. Pullman chuckled. "Dear? She a-asked you a question."

"Oh, sorry, what did you ask?"

Meagan repeated, "How much is the pay?"

"How, how much do you want?" King said wiping his forehead. The experience was draining his brain. She overwhelmed him, and he was sinking into quicksand in his mind.

Mrs. Pullman snickered out loud. "Name your p-price, honey! You've g-got him!" She doubled over in the club chair, laughing.

Meagan could feel the heat of embarrassment plastered on her face. Her armpits threatened to light her sweater on fire with the stress of her situation. She was unprepared for the effect the kind man and his perfect teeth and the aroma of seasoned pork would have on her. Meagan knew that if Rhonda saw the way Mr. Pullman filled his jeans, she would kidnap him and tie him up.

"Incredible." Mrs. Pullman murmured shaking her head at the hilarious scene before her. "Sa...sweetheart, be careful, that blushing just makes you even prettier. King m...might never recover!"

King spoke up, "Please ignore my mother. Will thirty thousand a year work for you?" If she said forty, he was ready to cough it up somehow, just to look at her every day. He wondered how many soft, form-fitting sweaters she owned; there might be an investment potential there; he could certainly see the value.

As she examined her circumstance, Meagan was suddenly so grateful that words escaped her. To work there; to hopefully eat his cooking and see his smiling face daily;

to help the delightfully honest Mrs. Pullman; to enjoy this country view; to collect the pieces of her family... All of this and he offered more money than she currently earned at Appliance Warehouse and the B & B combined!

"When can I start?" Meagan asked, bolting to her feet with readiness.

"You can s...stay for dinner," Mrs. Pullman stated matter-of-factly. "My eldest s-son is an accomplished cook. Aren't you, dear? How t-tall are you, Meagan?"

King nodded his head and admired her shapely legs. "Yeah, stay for dinner. Herb and garlic pork loin, honey mustard sauce, vegetables..." His voice faded; he took a deep breath and wiped his forehead again. Good lord, what was happening to him? He felt foolish.

Meagan beamed. "I'm six feet tall. Dinner smells wonderful, thank you."

Ace swaggered into the living room. "What have I missed?"

Mrs. Pullman answered, "Ace, this is Meagan. She is King's n-new housekeeper."

Ace rubbed the afternoon nap from his eyes and looked Meagan straight in the face. "Okay. I guess this isn't weird. You can start by climbing in my bed before you make it!"

"Ace! That was uncalled for!" King growled. "I'm sorry, Meagan. He's unfamiliar with females ... er, ladies."

"No problem," she replied to King's apology.

Ace laughed. "Whatever dude. I don't see a bunch of ladies waitin' in line for you. She's your maid. Get real!"

Meagan was not impressed with Ace's temper and lack of respect for his brother, who was, after all, kind enough to not send her to jail. Clowns that act like Ace are a dime a dozen; Mr. Pullman, on the other hand, was different. She couldn't say exactly what made him more of a man, but it was something.

No man alive could make himself appealing to Meagan by insinuating he would enjoy sex with her. In her heart, she believed a man like that, could have sex with anything, and like it.

She had put men in their place before and hoped she would not lose this opportunity over 'irreconcilable differences.' Several salesmen at the appliance store tried to get her fired after she shut down their advances, with a bet that she could beat them arm wrestling. She won, and they didn't like it. Thankfully, the owner of Appliance Warehouse, Mr. Chang, had great instincts and suggested the fellows behave themselves. Eventually, the lusty men moved on to hassle women who were easier prey.

Jack Pullman threw the front door open, swept in, and kissed his wife. "Hello, all! Are you here for the job?" he asked Meagan.

"Yes. I think I've been hired."

"Y-you have," Mrs. Pullman assured her.

"Dad," King asked, "Will you take the gator and check on the animals? I need to get dinner on the table."

"I'll help," Meagan volunteered.

"I'll watch," smarted Ace.

"No, you won't, Acer. You can help me take my s-shoes off," Mrs. Pullman ordered.

The food aroma mixing with King's appealing, manly cologne was intense, and Meagan felt unstable. Walking carefully on her new heels, she set the table for five, and poured wine for King and Mr. and Mrs. Pullman; Ace preferred beer.

"Mmm, this pork is amazing! Where did you learn to cook, Mr. Pullman?" Meagan wondered.

"Thanks. I started cooking for survival in college and liked it. I thought about starting a restaurant, but the pawn business was a better fit for me. Would you like some wine? And please, call me King."

"No, I don't drink. I never have."

"That needs to change!" popped Ace. "Is she going to live here? I might have to move in!"

Meagan smiled kindly. She remembered when Paxton talked like that; back before the punching ... when he wasn't scared of her. "King, what kinds of animals do you have?" she asked innocently, making conversation.

"Alpacas. They were pawned. I paid fifty dollars a head for them. They seemed interesting and I like their coats, er, fleece."

"That donkey is doing a good job," Jack informed them. "He's an excellent watchdog."

King was somber through most of dinner. Mrs. Pullman concluded that, since King had never talked about a woman, he was mulling over his new hire. A helper is exactly what Mrs. Pullman thought her son needed since he was breaking into the ranching business. Along with all of King's other responsibilities; a maid was a wise decision.

Ace couldn't stop talking. He went on about a woman he met several years ago; how beautiful she was. When he exhausted his long list of female conquests, he switched to sports. His mother was familiar with the calculating look on Ace's face; it meant trouble, and Mrs. Pullman didn't want trouble between her boys.

After dinner, when King stood to begin clearing the table, Meagan jumped up to help, and Ace followed. At the sink, Ace set his plate down on the counter and pressed his hand to Meagan's ass. "Oh!" she yelped in surprise, raised her foot and stabbed her heel down into Ace's bare foot.

"OW! Shit!" Ace yelled. "What the hell?" He hopped around the kitchen checking his foot for blood.

"I'm sorry," Meagan apologized demurely. "I must have lost my balance." She continued scraping the plates.

Jack Pullman witnessed the ordeal and kept his mouth shut. He didn't approve of a fighting woman, but neither did he appreciate a rude man. Ace hobbled back to the table under King's disapproving glare. Since no one was badly hurt, King ignored the situation, and cleaned up the kitchen.

As Meagan was leaving, King walked her to the door. "Ms. Morris, it was nice to meet you," he said shaking her hand.

The feeling of his hand swallowing hers was a surprise. When he finally let go, she was dazed; everything about him was a revelation. "Thank you for a wonderful dinner. I will be here at eight am." Her sexy, new pumps elevated her to six-foot four, face to face with King. The stress and shame of gazing into his kind, blue eyes at close range was too much. She turned to leave, quickly skirting the driveway rocks.

King shouted, "You may want to wear different shoes!"

"Roger that!" she replied, waving from her truck window.

Jack fell back onto the sofa, rested his legs on the coffee table and admitted, "Well, I have to say, I'm not sure I would have hired her, King. She looks like trouble, but you made the decision and I'm good with it."

Mrs. Pullman poked her husband in the ribs. "She's fine, dear and s-she seems to need the job."

He listened to his parents' comments about Meagan, and shrugged." We'll see. She drives an eight-cylinder truck."

"Yeah, but those spikey shoes ..." Jack shook his head at the tall girl's odd choice in footwear.

Mrs. Pullman nodded her head in agreement with King. She understood the language of working country people. A truck signified labor and the Pullmans appreciated and were grateful for labor. "Oh, I think King liked those 'spikey s-shoes'?" she observed. "He could look her in the eye. Right, King?"

Her question went unanswered. She knew her son was conflicted. Something was bothering him, and she wished he would just say it. Instead, he scoured the sink, reflectively.

12 Hot Knotty Woman

Driving back to the Willowby's after dinner, Meagan texted Rhonda, "I need different clothes."

Excited about the big change in Meagan's career, Rhonda called her. "Did you get the job? Where is it? How's the pay?"

"Yes, I got the job. I'll be a housekeeper and personal assistant, and the pay is great," she confirmed. There was so much more that Meagan wished she could tell Rhonda. She dreamed of having no secrets with Rhonda. That meant telling her about the things that made Meagan's life feel full. Things that now were gone, like the ruby rose she had yet to reclaim. She would want to describe King, but she couldn't. Mr. Pullman protected her at his pawn shop and she would return the favor. This job, and getting her possessions back, was too important to be gossiping about her boss and how he made her sweat when he was near. "The atmosphere is good, and the people are nice," she acknowledged and fanned her steaming armpits with her free hand.

"Wow. I didn't know it was that kind of job."

This was the Rhonda that Meagan knew; the one who was passing judgment right then. Rhonda had five careers to Meagan's one. Her tone told Meagan that she was disappointed with her choice to work in someone's home rather than in the 'business world.'

"Are you going to have to … wipe someone's … you know …" Rhonda asked cautiously. She was glad Meagan couldn't see her rolling her eyes. Rhonda hardly ever changed Alex's diaper; she drove him to her mother's house. She did a great job with it. Just imagining the deed caused her gag reflex to spasm.

"Probably not," Meagan defended, "but for this job, I would."

"Maybe you should have gone into nursing. I didn't know you liked to help on such a personal level. Are we still good for tomorrow at eight?"

"Yes."

Meagan's driving matched her pensive mood as she slowly brought the truck to a stop at the B & B. It was too late to go shopping for the right 'first day of work' clothes, so she would have to wear whatever she could find in her closet until she could get to a store.

Morning arrived at the ranch. A note taped to King's front door made her smile. 'You don't have to knock. List of things that need to be done is on the counter.'

Not knowing what to expect, Meagan marched into the kitchen, rolled the sleeves of Paxton's shirt up to her elbows and checked that it was tucked in her jeans. Her jeans were much looser than they had been a month ago. As she mentally ran through the list of stressors in her life, it hit her that the only food she could remember recently, was what she ate at the Pullman house. She knew that to keep her muscles tight and healthy, she needed to focus more on eating and working out. It would have been devastating to her if Mr. Pullman fired her because he thought her too weak to handle it.

"A list!" she said, amused with Mr. Pullman's apparent affinity for note writing.

Grimacing in pain, Brenda Pullman leaned against the fridge. She studied Meagan at the kitchen sink. "King wanted to m-make sure you were all set." She glanced over at the note.

"Yes, he did. He left no stone unturned! Where is he?" Meagan inquired.

"The men are working in their shops today." Brenda moved to lean on the counter for balance.

Meagan noticed the elderly woman was only wearing a sock on one foot. "Ms. Brenda, let's go back to your room; I'll strip your bed and help you with your compression socks."

"Oh," Brenda replied. She did not expect the angelic woman to anticipate her needs. "That would be nice."

Once the bedding was in the washer and Meagan had assisted Ms. Brenda with her socks and hair, she discovered that the country woman hated to miss her television shows; Jeopardy and The Price is Right. When she wasn't watching her shows, she worked word searches. The way she struggled with her words occasionally frustrated her, but she did not give up and Meagan respected that. Coping with the aftereffects of a stroke could be maddening; Meagan's uncle Abe suffered that way.

Mr. Pullman's fridge was filled to the brim with an amazing array of items and prepared dishes. Meagan was beginning to realize what a planner the man was. When she opened a container of chicken salad she knew Mr. Willowby would die for the recipe; it smelled heavenly. Croissant rolls on the counter were perfect for sandwiches. While Meagan assembled everything, Mrs. Pullman added a bit of sugar to her pitcher of homemade sun tea.

Getting to know Mr. Pullman's mother was wonderful. While they ate lunch together, Ms. Brenda talked romantically about her youth and growing up in

Texas; Meagan could almost feel the west Texas wind on her skin. When Ms. Brenda couldn't fight back her yawning anymore, she excused herself to lie down for her afternoon nap.

Meagan washed and dried the dishes and put them away before sitting down in Mr. Pullman's living room to enjoy the view of the acreage. The alpacas were testing the donkey's patience with their antics. Her quiet time was disrupted by a knock at the front door.

A disheveled cowboy smiled charmingly at her, revealing bits of tobacco stuck to his teeth. "Miss, I got a delivery for Mr. King Pullman?"

Her curiosity piqued. "Okay, what is it?"

"Alpacas. You got a corral or something for 'em? This eighteen-wheeler 'ud make a mess a yer land."

"Ah, yes, sure," she said. "Your truck does look too heavy to drive on the pasture. I'll be right back." Meagan felt conflicted about leaving the house while Ms. Brenda was snoozing, however she couldn't ignore Mr. Pullman's delivery either.

"Okay, Miss."

Meagan jogged to the garage side door knowing exactly what she needed; rope. Stringing those animals together along one rope was no different than beading a necklace, she imagined, and she'd made plenty of those for extra money. She ran back to the trucker, toting a forty-pound coil of rope and yelled, "Okay, let them out!"

Cowboy connected a heavy corrugated metal ramp to the backend of the truck for the animals to exit. "Yes, ma'am," he said, removing his weathered cowboy hat. He raised the roll-up door on the back of the semi.

Meagan approached quickly and was overwhelmed. At least five hundred chickens responded to the light and began clucking, which disturbed a gray and white donkey, which then upset a dozen llamas and alpacas. As chaos ensued, the cowboy waved Meagan up to the truck.

She climbed up the ramp and asked, "Which ones?" A nosy, female alpaca shoved her furry face in Meagan's ear allowing Meagan to quickly loop the rope around the nosy girl's neck

"These eight, fat woolies, ma'am," Cowboy said pointing them out to her. "The shaved ones go 'ta different rancher.

She froze. "Eight?" Megan was not one to back down from a challenge no matter how in over her head she was. For her boss, she would give it her best effort. With six feet of slack in the rope, she threw a loop around another jittery alpaca and talked herself through tying a second perfect Alpine Butterfly knot.

"Yes! Come on ladies and gentlemen," Meagan crooned in a singsong voice. Shaking out six more feet of rope, she executed another secure knot on a third alpaca.

Cowboy was amused. "In all my days, Lady, I ain't never seen no knot tyin' the likes 'a yourn!" He whipped out his cell phone to record Meagan tying knots around the remaining five anxious animals while she sang. "Holy crap! You did it!" he shouted excitedly. In all the racket, Meagan didn't notice Cowboy laughing so hard he could barely breathe.

"Hold these last four in rope order," she ordered and scurried down the plank with the first four animals while Cowboy methodically released the last four to follow.

"Thank you!" she yelled as she jogged to the side of the house toward the main corral. "Did Mr. Pullman pay you?"

"Yup. Bye, now," he shouted, smiling and shaking his head in disbelief. Initially, he thought she was going to ask him to carry the fat buggers to the corral. There was no way that was going to happen. Nope. Instead, he was sure he had just captured the next viral You Tube video.

Ace and Jack put in a full day of work in their shops. King left Marty in charge, so he could go home early and pound some nails in the second-floor addition before bad weather might hit. Driving was so natural to King that he never remembered the trip because of the detours his mind took while he was at the wheel. There were many times King was genuinely surprised when he made it home. The mental detours helped him sort out his troubles even though he missed smelling the roses of the journey.

Ace had gone back to his own house, much to King's relief. He loved his brother, but around Meagan, he resembled a dog in a rut. King was okay with Ace's return to his house, so long as he beefed up his security system. Together, they installed camouflaged night vision, motion sensor cameras that covered every side of his house, and a naval horn that could be heard two miles away. Hopefully, the two men mysteriously shot in King's house would stay away.

Steering his truck toward the ranch, he thought about his new domestic employee. She seemed too perfect and that had his radar blipping.

"Oh, oh, she's gone," he mumbled. Meagan's truck was not in his driveway, and it was only four in the afternoon. She was supposed to stay until 5:30. He felt a stab of panic for his mother who could not be left alone.

She had shown up for work, the note on the front door was gone. He hurried into the house shouting, "Mom? Meagan?"

No answer. "Damn." King felt his phone vibrating through the thin, leather jacket lining. "Hello?"

"King, it's Dad. Your mother had a fall. I'm here with her at the hospital."

"Oh. Is she going to be okay? How bad was it?" King asked worriedly. Pink sweater's first day on the job had rapidly become a mess.

"She's gonna be fine. I fired that 'maid.' I know she was a looker, son, but I didn't trust her. If she had been in the house, your mother wouldn't have fallen. She was clearly irresponsible. I'm going to look for someone new; maybe from an agency."

His jaw went slack. King knew his father was smart to not trust the strange, beautiful woman who answered the ad, but it all happened so fast. "Yeah, hmm, you're probably right. We really didn't know her. When will Mom come home?" There was no point to arguing with his father over Meagan even though he did not feel relieved about her having been fired.

"Tomorrow morning. She has a sprained ankle. By the way, thanks for loaning out Storm," Jack added, "he's a great dog. He eats a lot, but he hasn't shit in the store."

"And he won't, so long as you and Mr. Lee don't forget about him. Are you bringing Mom back here tomorrow?"

"Yes, if that's okay. She eats better at your house."

King was satisfied with the decent report on his mother. Despite her fall and the fact that he just lost the prettiest thing that ever graced his doorstep, he could now concentrate on the upstairs addition. It more than bothered him that he misjudged Meagan, which put his mother in danger. Maybe he was losing his discernment ability with people and that worried him. In his line of work, reading people accurately was essential.

Sorting through his deep freeze, he pulled out a shrimp and sausage medley he made several weeks ago. There was plenty of time to work while it cooked in the oven. He donned a tool belt and proceeded to put some walls up on the addition.

Hours later, King was forced to stop working. It had gotten dark. The sun went down, and he never noticed; he had been so engrossed hammering nails into sheetrock. He used the bottom of his t-shirt to wipe the sweat from his face and neck and surveyed his building progress.

With twenty minutes left on the casserole, he drove the gator out to check on his animals. He had asked Meagan to do that...but she probably didn't. As he made his way to the alpaca's corral, his heart rate jumped at the number of animals; it had more than doubled. He was stunned.

"What the dickens?" he muttered to the curious faces approaching him. "How? Well, hello there Nosy." The tallest of the new group of alpacas was a friendly girl. She boldly poked her head at King's chest and was rewarded with a good head rubbing. He scrutinized the fields for tire tracks through his land and there were none. "Hmm."

He made a quick phone call to Dawson's Delivery Service.

"Yeah, Mr. Pullman, I done dropped those woolies off earlier this afternoon," reported the cowboy.

King was stumped. "How?"

Cowboy stopped laughing long enough to share. "Well, that pretty wife a yourn, she's something. I'm a send you the video. It's great." King heard him fidgeting with his phone while speaking.

Wife? The pieces came together. King realized Cowboy thought Meagan was his wife, and that Meagan handled the animals... and there was a video. "What video?"

"I jus sent it. I gotta go. Thank ya fer your business, Mr. Pullman."

"Sure," King responded absently. He wandered into the barn office, eager for a place to sit down and process the information about Meagan. He tapped play.

He had not seen this Meagan; she was a country girl in the video. Her worn jeans and plaid shirt suited her, he thought. Her hair was in a ponytail on the top of her head and she was roping his livestock! "What?" He grabbed a pair of reading glasses and leaned in to his phone to see her better. She cooed to the alpacas as they spouted their guttural bleating. Meagan smiled and sang while the tall one kept nuzzling her neck. Another nuzzle, and an ear lick. That crazy alpaca had a long tongue! Meagan cheered because she had apparently remembered her knot tying skills, then she roped another. A nearby male alpaca didn't care to be that close to her and spat at her face. "Oh no! Ha, ha, ha!" King couldn't keep himself from laughing. Meagan's face was covered in undigested fragments of grass and spittle, while Friendly Girl had Meagan's ponytail in her mouth! Meagan's eyes were huge as her head was jerked back, but she hung on and continued to sing; refusing to let go of her crazy knot-tying scheme on the sixth creature. "Oh, no. Oh my God, this is funny! Ha, ha." King scrolled down and noted the video aptly named, 'Hot, Knotty Woman with Woolies', had over ten thousand views.

He smiled proudly. "So, Meagan roped them so she could corral them for me. What an industrious woman." Pride surged through King and with it, a renewed zeal to find Meagan and re-hire her. Apparently, Jack didn't learn the reason Meagan was not in the house. Any woman who was as resourceful as Meagan, well, she shouldn't have been fired. "I don't care how pretty she is," he stated, as he threw on his old college hoodie. He had to get to her before the night was gone. As soon as he had her address off her application, he was hitting the road to straighten things out.

13 Go Get Her

His anxiety over apologizing to Meagan as soon as possible messed with his rationale; he should have showered. He should have eaten, for that matter. He was lucky he remembered to turn off the oven. If he had thought it through, as he did with other areas of his life, he wouldn't have chased Meagan down while he was starving, and smelled like sweat and lumber.

Blanchard Avenue was not well lit, but thankfully the three-story Victorian B & B was hard to miss. He rolled into the small parking lot in front of the building and took a deep breath. He was about to lose his nerve when he noticed lights coming down the driveway from the back of the building. It was the big, brown truck. The decision to follow her was simple.

Meagan snaked down Blanchard and turned onto Highway Ninety for several miles before exiting on Northwest. King kept a discreet distance, but he bet she was too preoccupied with where she was going to notice his headlights behind her.

"Hmm, The Electric Panda." He had never heard of the establishment, but apparently, a lot of other people had. The place was hopping and Meagan had no choice but to park in the far, back corner and hike to the bar. Watching

Meagan walk alone through the huge parking lot in her wispy dress, with her glossy hair down in waves, stressed King out. She appeared completely unaware of her vulnerability. King knew her peril was real. He waited until she was inside the building before pulling his truck up to the valet. He tossed the attendant his keys then slipped inside The Electric Panda.

The wait staff were dressed in white; giving the place a clinical air. King could have been mistaken for an air conditioning serviceman in the sterile bar. Talking was impossible with music so loud the floor vibrated. Places like that weren't for talking and King knew it. The sleek people here were done talking. They wanted action.

Suddenly, the music stopped and a throng of people clapped. As he traveled farther into the monstrous room, he realized the music was live. The DJ announced, "Registration is closed! Five minutes until the contest! Back for more abuse, here is Don Canter with a song by Dreadfully Dead. Show him some love!"

A handful of people applauded and someone yelled, "Sing it, Captain."

It was a raised stage suitable for a star.

King decided to hang back by the bar and listen to Don sing. Following Don, an older woman, built like a man and sporting a fur vest, belted out, 'A Bridge over Troubled Water' the way 'Disturbed' sang it. She did a great job with it, in King's opinion; for a karaoke club, the talent was impressive.

The dim atmospheric lighting was sufficient to make Meagan's blond hair glow like an angel's. King could easily track her from his seat at the bar. "Jack and Coke," he called to the bartender.

Meagan embraced a red-haired woman and King assumed they were friends.

"Thanks Don, and thank you Lisa!" The DJ announced, "To start things off, please welcome, Meagan Amber!"

King nearly choked on his drink.

There was a disagreement between Meagan and her friend as the friend pushed Meagan to the stage. She reluctantly climbed the stairs, encouraged by the crowd. The bartender stopped his work to see what Meagan would do. The redheaded friend used sign language to communicate with the indignant DJ then scurried to the stage and handed Meagan a small, black guitar. The crowd cheered wildly with anticipation as she snuggled comfortably under the guitar strap.

King's heart was hammering in his chest; he was at war with himself. The desire to sweep Meagan out of this place battled his concern and morbid curiosity about her performance, not to mention his analysis of her name. "Something about her name..." he mumbled.

She strummed and purred into the mic, "How are you all doing tonight?" The crowd responded with whistling and cat calls. "That's what I thought," she added, causing a surge of laughter. The long fingers of her left-hand curled around the neck seamlessly reaching notes and chords with ease. She smiled. "Beatles for you tonight."

The DJ stood, arms crossed like a sentry at the palace gate. King gathered that he was not too pleased with Meagan's command of the stage. It wasn't karaoke. It was real, and it was all her.

King held one finger up to the bartender who quickly responded with another Jack and Coke, and commented, "She's hot. Do you know her?"

"Huh?" King heard the bartender, but his eyes were riveted on Meagan. "Yeah, I know her." Radiant, was the word King was looking for; she looked radiant. "So," he checked, "you haven't seen her in here before?"

The bartender shrugged his shoulders. "Nope, I would have remembered her. A babe like that? Whew..."

What the thirty-year old bartender with plugs in his earlobes thought about Megan, shouldn't have irritated King, but it did. The leggy beauty on the stage corralled eight alpacas all by herself—she was not the girl for 'Lobes'—in his opinion.

It was subtle, but as Meagan glanced out over the crowd, her countenance changed. It was as though a completely different person just took over her body and the real Meagan left the building. Astonished, King wondered if anyone else saw what he did. Her fingers sailed over the frets; delighting every ear with her version of George Harrison's song, 'My Guitar Gently Weeps.'

If he hadn't been watching Meagan with his own eyes, he would not have believed that voice belonged to her. The clear, resonant vocal tinged with a hint of tears, shoved the arrow a bit deeper into his heart. When she strummed the last chord, King wiped his forehead, downed the remainder of his drink and slapped thirty dollars on the bar with a salute to the barkeep.

Back in his truck, he texted her, "Meagan, thank you, for what you did today. Please come back to work. You're on my payroll, not Jack's. Mom gets released from the hospital tomorrow, and she would like it if you were here."

He set the phone on the passenger seat in his truck and steered back to the ranch, lost in thought. This time he was trying to unravel the confounding puzzle that was Meagan. "Meagan Amber, hmmm." There was a strange familiarity about that name.

Andrew stood at his second-floor bedroom window, frowning at the morning fog. He sipped his latte and waited to see pretty Meagan scurry to her truck. Since his room was directly under Meagan's and the floor squeaked, he was alerted to her comings and goings. She promised she would meet him for dinner at Angelo's Italian restaurant, Friday evening. The thought of cruising with Meagan in his convertible Corvette sent a shiver of excitement through his body. He knew they would have a great time and it would end with a kiss. He had imagined that kiss, and where it would lead, so many times since she moved in.

In the past few years, his focus had been on creating avenues of wealth for himself. Andrew couldn't recall the last real date he had. At that juncture, he concluded, if the wait was all for Meagan, it was worth it. Reaching for his IPad, he searched beach vacation packages; that was the obvious way to get her in a bikini.

"What was that all about?" Meagan shouted, inches from Rhonda's face. "Huh? Since when do you think I can sing…or play a guitar? That, in there, on that stage…could have been a disaster!" Meagan yelled above the noisy, drunken, happy hour mob.

Rhonda had never known Meagan to spit fire like that. "I'm sorry…but I'm not! Look Meg, you are so much more than a desk job or a caretaker! You have real talent. A few times when we were kids—you thought I was going somewhere—I didn't. I sat on the floor outside your bedroom door and listened to you play."

"Why? You had no right. You were spying! Is this really because my choice of employment embarrasses you?"

Rhonda defended her position. "What? No! I knew you would never actually play your music for my parents or me because all your songs were about sadness and loss… and I don't blame you. But they were beautiful and sometimes you would start crying when you sang. I cried too. You have real talent and I'm sorry I waited over twenty years to tell you!"

Meagan softened. "Whose guitar is this?"

"My son's. He doesn't know I borrowed it."

"Excuse me," Meagan shouted. Her phone buzzed with a text from King.

"Meagan, thank you for what you did today. Please come back to work. You're on my payroll, not Jack's. Mom gets home tomorrow and she would like it if you were here."

Meagan responded, "Thanks, I will be there."

"Who is it?" Rhonda snooped.

"My new boss. I should go. I have to be at work early." Emotionally drained from her performance and frustration with Rhonda, she was done with The Electric Panda.

14 Discovery

The scent of freshly ground coffee wafted through King's tidy kitchen. Ms. Brenda hobbled in on a walker. "I am s-so glad you came back, Meagan! I'm the first to admit, Jack's temper can make him unreasonable sometimes. How are you, dear?" she inquired.

"I'm glad to be back, thank you. Your speech is doing great! How is your foot?" she asked. Her peripheral vision caught movement out by the barn; King was working with the animals.

Brenda smiled. "My ankle will be fine. You know, we were both so harried yesterday. I want to ask you; how is it you carried me, like a man, to your truck and into the hospital?" she earnestly inquired. "I think it was a miracle."

"Well, I work out regularly," Meagan shared nonchalantly. "Let me help you get your socks on and we'll have breakfast, and then go visit the alpacas."

"Sounds lovely."

In the barn, King attempted to use his new clippers to sheer an alpaca for the first time. Nosy Girl seemed the most agreeable to the process. She calmly stood, muzzled in the corner of a stall in the barn while King meticulously zipped off her fleece.

By the time Nosy Girl was devoid of her fluff and returned to the pen, Meagan and Ms. Brenda appeared in the gator; much to King's amazement. "Not the girl for Lobes…" he muttered. The gator had a tricky gear shifting system, which Meagan obviously figured out.

"Hi." He smiled and waved. A mere four feet from the corral, Ms. Brenda elected to stay in her seat. "Nice to see you both," he greeted with a wink to Meagan.

"Thank you," she mouthed.

"Oh, dear, these animals are b-big!" Brenda exclaimed. "Are they dangerous?"

King stifled a laugh remembering Meagan's interaction with the alpacas. "Not really. None of these are over a hundred and eighty pounds and generally are not aggressive.

"She looks good," Meagan complimented, nodding toward the friendly, freshly shorn animal.

King explained his struggle with some of the alpacas, "They are ornery and somewhat skittish… except the tall, frisky girl; she was agreeable." he winked at Meagan again, turning her face beet red.

Brenda enjoyed the fact that her son seemed more alive than she had ever seen him. His eyes sparkled as he talked about his alpacas and the ranch.

Driving past King's house, Gayla noticed a strange, clean truck with a bumper sticker that read, 'Girls love trucks too.' It was parked next to King's. She knew the vehicles associated with King's business and family; that brown truck wasn't one of them. Her mind would not accept the idea of another woman. She had to find out. She slammed the gearshift into park and sprinted into King's house.

"Hello?" she shouted, marching to the windows. King was in the distance, down by the animals. "There are definitely women here," she snarled. In a flash, she was running through the pasture, full bore. "What the hell, King?" she screamed.

Brenda Pullman's hand covered her heart, distressed that the woman was yelling at King. She leaned over to Meagan and whispered, "Will she hurt him?"

"Ah... I hope not," Meagan answered, surprised. King was an intelligent, tall, strapping man with obvious strength, yet Mrs. Pullman was worried for his safety. "Hmm."

Gayla jerked open the corral gate, yelling, "Who is she?" and pointed to Meagan.

"You have no business here, Gayla. I have already told you that!" King snapped.

Gayla lunged toward King and slugged him in the neck, sending him backward to the fence. Donkey scurried over, spun a half turn, and caught Gayla on the ass with a hard, fast hoof, causing her to turn and twist her ankle. She grabbed her rear, wailed in pain, and hopped on one foot, screaming, "You hurt me, King!" Then she fell.

Nosy Girl spat a meaty wad of cud directly at Gayla's face.

"Ew! Shit!" she screamed in disgust, wiping the slime from her eyes and wincing in pain.

"We can take you to your car," Meagan offered.

"My car? I can't sit down, you idiot! I need to lie down! I'm bruised and my ankle is broken!" She rubbed her sore posterior as King helped her off the ground.

"Get in," Meagan ordered Gayla. This was the first time in her life Meagan had witnessed a man not defend himself at all against a woman. She couldn't understand why he didn't even put up his guard. Mrs. Pullman's concern was valid; maybe her son couldn't defend himself; maybe, he never learned how, Meagan reasoned. There were men who only knew how to use a gun; she assumed King would be the kind of man who knew how to do it all. She guessed wrong.

Gayla lay on her side in the bed of the gator whimpering, while King felt her ankle for damage. "You scraped the skin. You'll be fine," he assured her, then, informed Meagan and his mother, "I'll be done in a couple of hours." Meagan noticed King feeling around his neck and stretching his head from side to side as though he was trying to correct something. He was in pain.

"No, I won't be fine. You owe me!" Gayla bellowed in outrage.

In the house, Gayla hobbled straight to the master bedroom and sprawled out on King's bed, yelling for an ice pack for her ass.

While Ms. Brenda and Gayla took an afternoon nap, Meagan searched the kitchen drawers for the ruby brooch. No luck. Since the old man brought the piece to King, she felt sure King had it, and she would find it, soon.

She paused at the kitchen window with her glass of tea and watched King check the corral fence. When he paused to wipe his face, Meagan filled a large tumbler with frosty tea and drove it out to him.

He saw her coming and flashed a grin; it was addictive, she thought. Every time he smiled, she wanted another one. "I thought you might like this."

He took the glass and sat down on a bale of hay, craning his neck again and wincing.

Meagan slid out of the gator and walked to him. "Want some help with your neck?"

"Only if it doesn't involve a rope," he said. There was that grin again.

She melted and smiled back. "No, it doesn't. If you can lie down flat, it would help."

King was game for anything that would bring him some relief. When Gayla punched him, he heard something pop in his neck. He had been feeling a stab in his upper back every time he turned his head. He set the tea on a nearby hay bale then laid down on a patch of grass by the barn, and announced, "I'm ready!"

"Okay," Meagan responded dropping to her knees at his head. They peered at each other upside down.

She reached under King's upper back and pushed her fingers up in a massaging motion. He groaned. "How do you know what to do, Meagan?"

"My best friend's dad was a Chiropractor and I watched him do this. Just relax," she urged and continued massaging until it was clear King was relaxed. His eyes were closed and his body felt like putty in her hands. Her fingers traveled up toward his well-muscled neck and stroked hard and long for several minutes. King sighed contentedly as her hands cupped the sides of his head. He wasn't expecting what happened next.

She pulled hard; stretching his neck. His eyes flew open when his neck popped twice, then Meagan let go and patted his shoulder. "All better!" she informed him.

King was certain he was paralyzed. He laid there, eyes closed, motionless, and deeply concerned. He checked for movement in his extremities and when everything felt operational, he slowly moved his head from side to side; no pain. When he finally glanced up to thank her, Meagan was halfway back to the house. "Lovely Meagan Amber," he spoke to the sky, "she ropes alpacas and brings beauty, music, and healing."

Yes, she did do that, and it was great, but it was what she wasn't doing, that was getting under King's skin. She wasn't falling all over him. In his entire life, he only had to imagine a woman kissing him and the universe converged ... and it happened. Something was going awry. During her interview in the pink sweater, he couldn't stop himself from imagining her kiss.

Meagan had ignored his mother and marched over to him. "Thank you for hiring me," she said dreamily, and planted a juicy, probing, and seductive kiss on his lips. When he began to sweat uncomfortably, he changed the vision and pictured Gayla's face; then he could hear what Meagan was asking.

He picked his tea up and gulped it gratefully, wondering how he could step up his game and make his vision a reality. "Hmm."

She patted herself on the back for being able to help her nice boss and immediately began her maid duties. After expertly cleaning the bathrooms, she slipped into King's office to check Drakeslist again for her possessions. There were a million things for sale on that website, and it was getting late. She zeroed in on a posting of a pheasant. Focusing on the details, she whispered, "Bingo."

King shucked his boots in the mudroom and quietly headed to his room. "Damn," he moaned. The last person he wanted to see in his home was Gayla, and she was lying on his bed. In his stocking feet, he approached the guest room his parents were using; no sign of Meagan or Brenda. Someone turned on a water faucet in the guest bathroom, but it was a ticking sound that captured his attention; he tiptoed to his office.

Meagan was at his computer, engrossed. She sat with her back to King. He instinctively took out his phone, held it up high and quietly snapped a photo of the screen she studied. He disappeared before she noticed he was there.

A sound of something falling in the bathroom alerted Meagan, and she wrapped up her investigation in a second, to check on Ms. Brenda.

She had dropped a can of hairspray into the bathroom sink.

"Let me comb your hair back for you, Ms. Brenda," she offered. Meagan took the brush from the sweating, stressed, elderly lady. Patiently, she brushed Brenda's thick, gray hair into a twist and secured it with a long barrette and a dash of hairspray.

"Thank you, dear. I napped all over that pillow today!" Brenda explained.

King stood out of sight; listening to their conversation. Brenda seemed to get along well with Meagan… what's not to like? King reviewed his few moments in her company, and it was absurd to realize that he knew virtually nothing about the beauty in his employ. Aside from some obvious talents she had, she was a stranger. His gut told him she was up to something. He knew he needed some answers, or he would never rest. He flipped his laptop open on the kitchen counter and turned the oven on to bake the chicken that had been marinating for hours. Foam, thick as a steak, crested the ale in his frosted beer glass; he sipped as he surfed the Internet.

He Googled, "Meagan Morris," and was shocked to learn that, under the name Meagan Calvert Morris, she had won boxing trophies at a well-known club in the city. The referee in the article was holding her hand in the air as the winner of the match against a Honduran woman.

It was the black skullcap…and the look of her mouth, covered in dried blood… Those lips resembled the brown lips of… Something niggled at his brain until it was painful. "Oh, my God! It's her—the robber woman with a gun! Holy shit, and she works for me now. I'm sure of it! This is insane!" A woman who had no issues pointing a gun at people would have no problem punching them. "Yeah, it's her." Taking a deep breath, King vowed to get to the bottom of it all. His mouth hung open over his unbelievably complicated situation; the thief from his shop, who shot the intruders in his home, was the same woman doing his mother's hair. The tingling sensation of being secretly watched by her in his bedroom turned to a creepy, stalker calamity.

An article about her husband, Paxton Calvert, stole King's attention. He was surprised to learn she was married, but more surprised that she was widowed and hadn't remarried. "Meagan, what are you trying to do?" he questioned the face on the screen. Remembering the baubles worn by the ladies in her photo, he suspected she was after the choker or the ring. "Maybe that ruby brooch?" he thought out loud. He was positive she had the cameo necklace since it was missing now, and she wanted another piece. Apparently, Jack hadn't come across any of the pieces yet; he hadn't mentioned anything.

King seriously doubted that Meagan would tell him the truth if he asked what she had been doing on his computer. His intuition steered him away from that conversation. Looking at his worried reflection in the oven door, he wondered if his growing fascination with Meagan was sick.

The timer on the oven beeped. It was time to insert the chicken and put wild rice on to cook as he continued to ponder Meagan. Should he trust her with his mother? The answer was, yes, because he knew she saved Ace when she shot the men who broke into his house. He considered asking her, point blank, if she shot Ace's attackers, but she would likely lie because she was in his house illegally at the time. A quick phone call to Officer Dell solved the mystery for King; ballistics had confirmed the bullets in Ace's assailants came from a nine-mm gun, like Meagan's

Another factor in his maid's favor was the fact that she fixed King's neck, and a nice person would do that. Truth was, he preferred being 'one up' on her. The fact that King was onto her and she didn't know it, he felt, gave him the advantage. His curiosity was at an all-time high as he enlarged the page on his laptop to get a good look at the photos he took behind Meagan's back. It was a photo of... a pheasant? "I thought she had better work ethic than to peruse the Internet on paid time." He smirked, wondering why a person who robs another at gunpoint would have ethics. "I'm an idiot, and she is shopping for a stuffed bird."

"Why would any woman want a taxidermy pheasant?" Totally bewildered by his discovery, he sat on the counter, tapping a spoon against his leg; thinking.

He texted the seller, "Still have the stuffed bird for sale?"

The answer came, "Sort of. Got someone looking at it tonight, I'll let you know if they don't show."

"If I could see it at the same time, you might get us bidding for it."

The seller responded, "Whatever; George Street Bakery parking lot, 9 pm. Cash only."

"Will do. Thanks," replied King.

He closed his laptop and took out his frustrations on the vegetables he was chopping.

15 Spilled Beans

"What are you cooking, King?" his mother asked, maneuvering her walker to the table near Meagan. "I used to cook."

"Chicken," King grunted.

Brenda's tone was nostalgic and touched Meagan. "What was your favorite dish?"

As Brenda shared her favorite recipes and their origins, Meagan washed her hands and set the table for the Pullman family. When all the water and wine glasses were filled, and the table was complete, Meagan announced, "It's five thirty." She gaped at King, flummoxed that he was so lost in his thoughts that he didn't hear any of Brenda's conversation or that it was five thirty.

"Hello?" Meagan asked again as she neared the spaced-out cook.

King shook off his thoughts. "Oh, did I miss something? I'm sorry. Yes, five thirty. See you later."

Jack arrived home from work and strolled into the kitchen to kiss his wife. "Hi, King," he said, with a scowl toward Meagan.

"She was just leaving," King informed him, wishing his father would not carry a grudge against Meagan.

Ms. Brenda waved to Meagan. "Bye honey."

Awakened from her lengthy nap, Gayla stomped into the living room and stopped abruptly before Meagan. “Who the hell are you? Who?” She snapped angrily, her hands on her hips.

“She’s King’s maid,” Brenda informed her. “I see you’re h-healthy.”

“Yeah, right.” She marched with a limp to the kitchen where King was serving up the food. “Which agency is she with?”

Guilt hammered at King. He met his father’s eyes; they both knew Meagan was not with any agency.

“Who are you?” Jack questioned the unknown female.

“Gayla. I’m Gayla. I’m King’s girlfriend.”

Jack’s eyebrows flew up in surprise. “Nice to meet you.” His eyes darted to King, looking for a denial of her statement.

“It’s ready,” King announced, ignoring the suspicious look from his father. “Dig in. That includes you, Gayla.

“It’s about time, King. Thank you,” she purred contentedly.

Meagan closed the front door quietly and walked to her truck, grateful that Gayla didn’t park behind her. She had more important things to do tonight than listen to Gayla beg King for money and attempt to have sex with him. She concentrated on the pheasant and the memory came alive.

She was six and had gone with her dad on a hunting trip. It was the one and only hunting trip they went on together. When she wasn’t playing with his phone, she was taking pictures with it.

Since her dad did not have a bird dog, Meagan knew she had to be vigilant and help her dad visually track the fowl once he shot it. It was a great stroke of luck that she had his phone set to movie. When Mr. Morris kicked up some underbrush, several large birds scuttled out and took flight. Meagan pressed 'record.' Her father took his best shot, which Meagan captured on film. Her effort was a huge success and her father took every opportunity to praise her. "Meagan was so clever to film the decent of the pheasant," he would tell people. "We watched the clip and it took us right to our kill." The best part for Meagan was the hug and pat on the head followed with, "I love you, Meggie."

"...And I'm home," she mumbled, aware that she had drifted down memory lane again. The Corvette convertible was not in the rear parking lot, which relieved Meagan; she wasn't interested in talking to Andrew. She had a pheasant mission to complete in a couple of hours. She took the stairs two at a time to her room. Meagan felt content lying on her bed, staring at the custom ceiling handiwork of an expert mason who had probably been dead a while.

Thoughts of Paxton returned. She had been having frequent 'Paxton thoughts' since moving into the Willowby B &B. "Maybe it's this place. It's old and probably haunted. I should have asked Aunt Agnes if anyone ever died in this house."

Sleep overtook her and she awoke in a panic twenty minutes before her meeting time with the seller of the pheasant. She peeled her work clothes off and donned the camo pants, black lace-up military boots, the AC/DC t-shirt, and Pax's leather jacket. No time to fiddle with overdoing her make-up for a better disguise, she grabbed sunglasses and a ski hat, and sailed down the creaky wooden stairs and out to her truck.

Brenda sensed King needed some space, so she sent him on a fake errand. "King," she spoke loudly for Gayla's benefit, "Your father needs a file from the shop. He's working on taxes. Would you be a dear and go get it?"

"Wah?" he muttered, concerned that his mother might be losing it and needed to see a doctor again.

She mouthed the words, "Go, now!"

King got the hint. He kissed her on the cheek and hurried to shower and dress to bid on a bird and, hopefully, not get shot by Meagan. "I need a Kevlar vest or a lobotomy," he whispered, adjusting the shower water temperature. If he could just get through the night alive, it would be a win.

Jack and Brenda sat in the living room, enjoying their after-dinner coffee. Brenda worked a word search puzzle book, while Jack manned the television remote looking for a good news station. Gayla occupied a club chair across from them. "So," she said, interrupting the mood. "Why did King hire that maid?"

"He has too much on his plate and needed the help," Brenda replied.

A thousand times, Gayla had fantasized about the day King would introduce her to his parents. It was always a sweet vision and she always felt proud. Not now. This was going terribly. No one had spoken at the dinner table except to compliment King on his cooking ability. Gayla thought she and King would grow closer over the years, but the past year had been anything but close. Her patience was running out, and earlier, that woman, or maid, or whatever she was, got on Gayla's last nerve. There was something between she and King, Gayla sensed it and loathed it. It needed to stop. She was going to put the brakes on it.

"Is it okay if I call you Mom and Dad?" Gayla asked.

Jack's eyes cut suspiciously over to his son's guest. "Why? You can call me Jack."

"And I'm Brenda."

"Well, I thought since King and I have a child together, we should start acting like a family," Gayla drawled innocently. "Right?

Brenda's eyes darted to her husband; she was concerned about his blood pressure. The information about their eldest son having a child was a shock. If the nervous, accusing woman before them wasn't careful, she might be the recipient of Jack's scalding temper.

"How old is your child?" demanded Jack.

"Twelve," she said, beaming. "He looks like King...and you."

There was something... it was years ago...a story, maybe a rumor that was gaining traction in Brenda's memory. She cocked her head inquisitively. "What's your last name?"

"Adamson, why?"

"What do you do for a living?" Jack persisted, as though any second Gayla would change her story and some other poor sonofabitch would be named the father.

"I'm a veterinarian," she responded.

Something was off, according to Brenda. The little hairs standing at attention on the back of her neck added to her discomfort. "Did you attend the University of Tennessee?"

"Yes." Gayla was pleased that King's parents were familiar with her education. "Did King tell you about it?"

"No, he didn't. I can't remember exactly who told me. I seem to recall hearing about you and your aspirations, when I worked at the bank."

Gayla shifted uncomfortably in the chair. "What did you do at the bank, Mom?"

"Not too much. I worked there for four years to help with King's college costs. He worked so hard, you know, I wanted to help. I managed some personal accounts for wealthy clients of the bank and assisted with financial planning. As we sit here and talk, more of it comes back to me," Brenda said pensively.

Gayla shot to her feet. "Okay then, Mom and Dad, I'm going to head home, to your grandson and I'll talk to you tomorrow!" She collected her boots on her way out the door.

"Funniest thing..." Jack growled, "Brenda, did you notice she didn't limp. There's nothing wrong with that girl, physically. What do you know about her?"

"Nothing really, I just have a feeling, dear." Brenda strongly suspected that King was in a mess, but before saying anything definite, she needed to check on her old information.

King walked back into the room, freshly showered and yanking an old college hoodie over his head, told his parents, "I don't know exactly what time I'll be home. Please don't wait up." He cautiously peered around the room, looking for Gayla.

Jack cleared his throat, "Your 'girlfriend' went home."

"Oh, good, she is not my girlfriend. Never was."

"King, do what you need to do." Brenda said calmly. "We love you."

16 Fowl Play

The George Street Bakery closed hours before King arrived.

"My God, it really is you!" he exclaimed, when he spotted Meagan's dark truck pulling up to the bakery to wait for the seller to show. Her windows were tinted dark; there was no way to see who was behind the wheel. He slowed his Ford pick-up and parked at the adjacent Hair Salon business. With numerous vehicles between them, King snuck out and edged closer to Meagan's vehicle then hid behind a minivan to observe.

A small SUV whipped into the parking lot. King felt his chest constrict when Meagan stepped out of her truck. "Shit!" he whispered. She was in her military clothing again, and her hands were in her pockets. "Not good." She had a swagger that she didn't have when she had robbed him. King assumed her thieving confidence was increasing as she got better at it.

A young man wearing sneakers and smoking a cigarette was carrying the foul. "You here for the bird?"

"Yes," she replied. "Set it on my tailgate, please."

"Okay," he agreed.

King couldn't take it another moment. He dashed to her as she pulled out the gun. His hand clamped down on hers, causing the weapon to fire into the air.

He pressed himself against her back, bracing her to him with one arm sealed around her arm and waist. Meagan couldn't move; his body was like a vice grip. King had her trapped where she stood. Of all the insane things to think about in that moment, King wished he were dancing with Meagan. For a moment, his mind saw her in a sleek black gown, with her hair down; he was in a tux and they were dancing, like lovers do.

Then the screaming began.

"What the hell, lady? Don't kill me!" yelled the seller. His hands were in the air and the cigarette bobbed from his lips.

"Then you better go, you rotten thief! That pheasant was never yours!" Meagan shouted. "You stole it!" She wanted to scream loud enough to shatter glass and deafen King. She stomped on his foot and only bruised her heel on the steel re-enforced toe of his work boot. His hot breath was steaming her ear through her knit cap and driving her mad. He was dominating her, which was a first for Meagan.

"Whose bird is it?" King gritted.

She was astounded that he caught her red-handed, trying to get her father's pheasant back; how he found out was a mystery to her. "Mine. It's mine," she replied, breathing heavily.

"Just like the cameo necklace?"

"Yes."

The young man peeled out as he flew out of the parking lot away from Meagan.

"What else?" King demanded turning her to face him. "What else are you going to risk lives for?" He braced her arms behind her.

"Daddy's silver pocket-watch, my punching bag," she admitted slowly, "and my guitar. I was robbed! Aunt Opal's..."

"Opal neck ribbon?" he finished with a nod of comprehension.

She nodded too.

He couldn't see her eyes through the dark sport sunglasses, but he knew she was on the verge of tears. King's mind spun a mile a minute over her mission to acquire the things she knew were hers. She hadn't mentioned the ruby brooch and it was in the picture she brought into his shop the day she robbed him. His voice went soft and kind, "Meagan, why are you working for me?"

She sucked in a deep breath, "I need the money, and I want my ruby brooch."

"Ah." He gave her back her gun. Why hadn't she at least pretended to care for his family? Her reasons for taking the job had nothing to do with the actual job. "See you in the morning," he said sorrowfully, and strode back to his truck. The beautiful, confused woman practicing vigilante justice over stuff he saw in his shop every day had tied King's heart in a knot—a painful knot.

Eyeing the pheasant on the passenger seat as she drove to the B & B, she attempted to sort out her feelings. How dare he insert himself into her quest! She was simply getting back the pieces of her life. Now that King knew her secret, surely, he would give her the brooch. She would then find a different job where people wouldn't follow her around. The fact that she didn't tell King the truth about her situation was coming back to bite her. But, how could she? Why would she have told him anything; it wasn't his business!

When she allowed herself to think about leaving her job as King Pullman's maid and Brenda's helper, it hurt. She saw King's face in her mind and heard King's kind voice in her ear; not to mention Brenda would be disappointed and at the mercy of whomever King hired next. There would be other jobs for her ... she had to stop giving King Pullman power over her. "No man needs to know the power they possess," Meagan reasoned, and texted King, "Don't follow me again."

He returned, "I don't care if you think it's your stuff, don't steal again."

"Am I fired, again?"

"Ah, shit," he moaned. Part of him wished she, her gun, and her problems wouldn't show up for work tomorrow. The other part of him hoped Meagan would stick with her job because he would worry about her if she didn't.

"No."

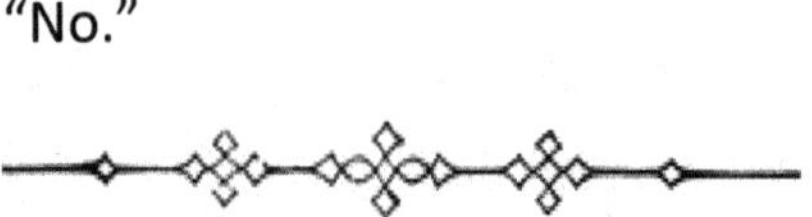

Peering out his second story window again, Andrew contemplated Meagan and her new job as she headed to work that morning in her heavy-duty truck. She was the first woman to capture his attention in a long time—with his parent's encouragement. In that morning's daydream, he imagined buying her a car. Since when should a woman like Meagan cart herself around in a man's vehicle? He planned to treat her like the lady she was, even though there had been times recently when he wondered if she even liked men. Yes, he would take her clothes shopping too; no more wearing her dead husband's fatigues. He would choose her clothes. Thinking about her prompted him to look at his new watch. His six-p.m. date with Meagan later that day could not happen fast enough.

17 Room for the Night

Squaring her shoulders and taking a deep breath, Meagan let herself in King's house at eight-thirty a.m. She texted him, "I'm here."

"With or without a weapon?"

She was not amused by King's snarky question. Surely, he knew she didn't carry a gun in his house. She responded, "It's in my truck. Am I fired?"

His maid was not one to be trifled with; the conversation felt full of fire. As he thought about her body pressed against his, the night before, he knew it was time to throw a little water on the flame. It was important that she come to King. He wanted her to kiss him, so he could kiss her back; childish as it was. "Hmm." His quandary was how to bait her, she wasn't like any other fish.

"No, you're not fired. My mom likes you and you're the only ranch hand I have. Please stay."

"No note today?" she texted smartly.

She completely blew off his begging, with not even a 'thank you' for not being fired. "Miss my notes?"

"No," she snapped back irritated, but she couldn't put her finger on exactly why she was irritated. This sarcastic side of King was different. She had never known a man like him. She wondered what else he had up his sleeve.

"Okay, good. I'll be home at three to work on the house," he replied, ending their text jousting.

Meagan tapped on Jack and Brenda's bedroom door. "Good morning!" she said and knelt before Brenda to take over the chore of putting on her compression socks.

"Good morning. Thank you dear. It's just us for breakfast. Jack and King have gone to work in the shops. Can we take a walk today?"

"Absolutely," Meagan responded, elated that Ms. Brenda enjoyed the outings to see the alpacas as much as she did.

Watching Meagan across the table during their morning meal, Brenda stirred her coffee and set her spoon down. "Meagan, tell me about you," she requeste.

"Hmm, well," Meagan began. "I'm fairly boring. I was an average student in school; average athlete on the track team; average decade-marriage to an average guy. He died in Afghanistan almost two years ago."

"Dear, there is nothing 'average' a-about you! For some reason, you just don't see it, which astonishes me." Brenda shook her head, disappointed with the people in Meagan's life that did not help her know her value. She set a warm, wrinkled hand on Meagan's. "You are an amazing woman, and I want t-to know what you plan to do with your life."

"I'm working here, and I'm getting myself together—alone," she stated.

"That is hardly a plan for the future! You need to dream! Dream about all the things that make you happy and bring you joy—great joy, Meagan. What m-makes your heart leap, dear?"

Getting my stuff back... But Meagan did not say that thought out loud. Her thoughts were interrupted by the recollection of King's text, commanding her not to steal again. "I'll let you know what I come up with, Ms. Brenda."

"I look forward to that."

While Brenda worked on her puzzles, Meagan sanitized the kitchen and bathroom counters, and then washed the kitchen floor before preparing a light lunch. A thorough search of King's fridge yielded ham and cheese sliders and soup.

"King never asks for help in the kitchen, even when I know he needs it," Brenda commented, stirring her homemade iced tea.

This conversation was new. Meagan listened while Brenda talked about the early days of her marriage and how King was a wonderful surprise, then how they planned for Ace. Her voice grew soft; her eyes distant.

A tapestry of the Pullman family formed for Meagan; it was rich with love and work.

When Brenda laid down for her afternoon nap, Meagan searched again for her ruby brooch. She had scoured King's closet and determined the brooch was not in there. Tomorrow, she would dig in some more closets. In the meantime, she found nothing of hers on Drakeslist. The frustration of her situation made her want to punch her stolen speed bag. "Pity the fool who tries to sell me back my own bag," she muttered, giving up her search temporarily when King appeared.

Disheveled and frustrated, Meagan looked up to see King. "I was just, just... tidying your room," she lied.

Her phone alerted her to a text from Andrew, "Hi. Bad news. Mom said to let you know a plumbing pipe broke. Two guests had to leave—no water. Plumber says it might be fixed by morning. Would you like to stay at a hotel with me tonight?"

"Uhgg. No!" She moaned in frustrated disgust.

"What is it?" King asked sensing she had just received bad news.

When Ace stayed at King's, he slept in the twin bed, in the child's room. Meagan wondered if King would mind if she used it for one night.

"Ah, would it be okay if I stayed here tonight? A pipe broke where I live. No water till tomorrow." She threw her hands up, exasperated. "I'll take the couch?"

"Ah," he nodded. King was surprised she asked. While his brain was adamantly saying no, his mouth said, "Sure. Use the baby's room." It couldn't hurt; it was just for one night, and his mother liked her.

"Thank you," she beamed. "I'll take care of the dinner you planned."

King was grateful for her offer; he needed to work on the addition. "Okay, well, excuse me," he said passing by her to get to his bedroom. He was glad he seasoned pieces of roast beef last night. Maybe she wouldn't screw it up.

Fresh from her long nap and feeling spryer than she had in a while, Brenda helped Meagan set the table early. They talked about the news they heard coming from the TV in the living room.

Meagan snooped around his kitchen and found all the ingredients necessary to surprise the Pullmans with homemade rolls to sop up the roast gravy with. The thought made her mouth water.

"Is someone at the door?" Brenda questioned when she heard odd noises coming from outside.

Meagan snickered. "No, King has been hammering on the upstairs addition for the last two hours. Do you know what that addition is going to be?"

"You know, dear, I have no idea. He just got it in his head that he needed an extra room. I think Jack is home," announced Brenda.

"He sure is, honey," Jack said, strolling directly to his wife for a hug and kiss. "She cooks?" he asked peering over at Meagan as she tossed flour around on the counter.

"Yes, she does," Meagan fired back. The oven beeped and she inserted a sheet of rolls and sent King a text, "Dinner is ready in fifteen minutes."

"On my way," he replied. The aroma of King's herb roast and vegetables wafted through the house. Meagan checked her watch and realized it was quitting time, but she didn't need to leave. She was glad; she would rather be there with Ms. Brenda than anywhere else, even with the irritation she felt towards King. Secretly, she thanked Aunt Agnes for her plumbing issues.

When King came in through the laundry room, Meagan was ladling stew into large bowls with dinner rolls on the side. His eyes scanned the length of her. King knew he should have talked to her about her clothes; he just wasn't sure exactly what he would say. She went from a seductive secretary in her soft pink sweater and short skirt at her interview, to sexy cowgirl in her jeans and plaid shirts. The more thought he gave the problem, the more it became a non-issue because there was nothing she could wear, save a tent, that would make her not appear seductive. That was the rub. She was too seductive and he shouldn't have hired her back; not to mention she was a vigilante. He knew he was a sucker.

Brenda informed him, "Home-made rolls by Meagan."

"Even better, I'll bet they'll be great with a little honey," he said with a smile. His thoughts about Meagan punching down dough for rolls were erotic. He recognized his visions were taking off in a ludicrous direction considering she probably couldn't stand him.

Meagan tried to ignore King, but his honey on the rolls comment ... she wondered if it was some sort of a double entendre. It made her sweat. The way he said it, felt provocative.

As they all sat down to enjoy their meal, the doorbell rang. King locked eyes with Jack; suspicious of who might be calling, he prayed it wasn't Gayla.

A slim thirty-year old man wearing lots of cologne asked, "Is Meagan here?"

18 The Pocket Watch

"Why?" probed King; craning his head for a better view of the Corvette in his driveway.

"We have a date. I'm Andrew."

"Oh," King smirked at the terrible start to this poor chap's date. "Come on in, you can join us for dinner." Never having been on an actual date in his entire life, King pondered the man's choice in clothing. He wore several layers of shirts topped with an army green, mountain climber's vest. His jeans were tight; they resembled denim skin. King noticed his reflection in the man's light brown, shiny shoes. "Hmm. Come in."

There was no way King was going to let Meagan out the door with this guy until he knew more about him. To say that King was thrilled with the opportunity to present Meagan with the dinner date she forgot was an understatement. He was giddy.

Jack and Brenda stopped eating and focused on the bizarre scene unfolding before them. King was grinning like he won the lotto as he watched Meagan's mouth move in slow motion. "Oh! Hi Andrew," she said, mechanically. "How did you find me?"

"I followed you here one day out of concern. Mom didn't even know where you were working! I'm glad I did follow you, because nowadays anything could happen," he informed her priggishly.

"That's true," agreed Brenda. "He's right a-about that. You never know."

Andrew added, "So, when you didn't show up for our date at the restaurant, I had to come here."

Meagan groaned. "Oh, right. Sorry."

He sat down at the table and studied Jack for a moment. "You look familiar."

"A lot of people say that," Jack responded. "What's your last name, Andrew?"

"Willowby."

"How did you meet Meagan?" inquired Brenda.

"Wow," Andrew laughed and shot a look at Meagan as she set a bowl of stew before him. "Did you arrange this inquisition?" No one else laughed. "We met at a family reunion when we were about fifteen," he disclosed. "I was adopted, so it's not like we're actually related. Technically, Meagan has no relatives except my mother, Agnes. They're all dead."

"Oh, dear!" Brenda exclaimed reaching to cover Meagan's hand with her own. "I'm sorry. I know..."

"I'm fine, thank you," Meagan whispered, squeezing Brenda's hand.

King knew she wasn't fine. She replaced people with things a long time ago and she wanted them back. She wasn't fine. She was delusional.

"I thought we could go see a movie," Andrew suggested. "The Assassin' is playing at eight." He refused to abandon what was left of their date. Knowing his parents were waiting on a report of his and Meagan's date, he didn't want to let them down.

Meagan shoved an oversized wad of beef in her mouth, buying precious seconds to consider his request. The fact that he followed her to work one day was weird; he distrusted her, like Paxton had.

Andrew remembered the fabulous antique watch recently given to him and dug it out of the side pocket of his canvas vest. He flicked the silver timepiece open to check the time. "This thing keeps perfect time," he said, smiling smugly and thinking himself a gentleman.

King's heart skipped a few beats when he noticed the alarming look in Meagan's eyes. "Nice watch, mind if I take a look at it?" asked King with feinted nonchalance, trying to avoid a possible murder in his home.

Jack cleared his throat. "Now I remember you!" he announced. "You tried to pawn that watch in my store."

"No, I'm sorry. I didn't go in your... pawnshop," Andrew stammered defensively.

The gut-wrenching pain etched in Meagan's face knocked the wind out of King. He examined the quality pocket-watch. Meagan turned it over in his palm and subtly pointed to the inscribed initials, "G.M."

"George Morris," she shared in a whisper.

"I'd like to own something like this, Andrew," King said. "Will you sell it?"

Meagan's eyes went wide and she was sweating again. How Andrew came to have the watch was an enigma. Her boss attempting to buy it was making the stress over the battle for the pocket-watch nearly unbearable.

Andrew smirked. "I don't think so, I mean, probably not. It was a gift and I should probably keep it."

"How about two hundred dollars?" suggested King. A guttural growl escaped Jack, indicating his disapproval of the transaction at their dinner table. From his point of view, King was losing it; he hired back that pretty, fake maid, had a child somewhere with a violent woman, and was now pawning at his dinner table. He needed to sit his son down and have a long talk with him, before King imploded.

King tried again, "Two fifty?"

"King?" Jack snapped, wondering what happened to King's reasoning ability.

"Ah, maybe three?" Andrew suggested with a cocky grin.

Meagan tried to jump up from the table to pummel the smart-ass thief, but King's vice grip on her forearm kept her in her seat.

Unnerved, over the poor business transaction in King's home, Jack shoved a forkful of dinner into his mouth and chewed with a vengeance.

Andrew watched King extract his money clip with hundred-dollar bills spilling out and changed his mind. "I think four hundred would be a fairer price."

Unable to tolerate another second of Andrew's thievery, Meagan lunged for him, and King wasn't fast enough to stop her. In one fluid movement, she came off her seat as her right fist shot straight into Andrew's face, knocking him backwards in his chair.

"Holy shit woman!" Jack yelled in a deep, pissed off tone, choking on his mouthful at the same time. "Are you okay, son?" he asked Andrew, coughing.

"He's not innocent!" Meagan defended herself. King's arm wrapped around her waist to keep her from finishing off her cousin.

"I think you should take the three hundred," Jack advised Andrew, then gave Meagan a reprimanding glare. "That was more than a fair offer."

"Shut up, you old fuck!" Andrew spewed as he regained his footing. "You wouldn't give me nearly what it's worth."

"You will not speak to these nice people like that." Every protective atom in Meagan's body wanted the rude cousin of hers on the ground. She twisted in King's arms and executed a perfect sidekick to Andrew's ribs, knocking him to the floor again.

Brenda clapped her hands together as though she bought a ticket for the fight.

Sufficiently defended and righted by the fighting woman, Jack helped Andrew off the floor. "You're leaving now."

"A word to the wise," King shouted to Andrew. "Do not, under any circumstance, touch anything—and I mean ANYTHING in her room. Understand?"

"Do you understand?" Jack double-checked, patting Andrew on the back. "You don't mess with our family."

"Ha! She's not your family! She's no one's!" Andrew shouted, wiping blood from his cheek.

Brenda stood. "Just a moment, Jack. I want to s-say something to this ignorant young man. A-Andrew, that special, beautiful woman," she informed as she pointed an arthritic finger at Meagan, "has more character in her pinky than you will ever know. She is caring and helpful, industrious and creative. She is precious to us and we now understand how precious we are to her. Thank you for bringing me a daughter. You can throw him out now, dear."

King felt a lump in his throat at the realization that Meagan was as fiercely protective about his family as she was about any of the 'things' she hunted. Still holding her to him, he leaned down to her ear, his lips touching her silky hair, he begged, "If I buy you a guitar, will you stay?"

Brenda overheard King and quirked her head in surprise. She knew she heard King mention a guitar to Meagan, just then, but she didn't know why. King had never cared about learning a musical instrument or even listening to the radio. He had always worked his tail off chasing the almighty dollar ever since his senior year in high school.

Meagan's emotions were all over the map. She peeled King's fingers from her waist, and then ran to the bathroom to cry in private. In her entire life, she had never been offered a bribe so painful. She knew what a wonderful man King was and the fact that he felt he needed to lure her to stay—with a guitar—was too much. She sat on the commode bawling. Her heart wanted to tell King that she didn't need a guitar to stay. On the other hand, she was pissed and wanted the classic Martin guitar given to her by her uncle. It was only right.

Brenda and King cleaned up the dishes and straightened the kitchen while Jack took his bourbon outside and sat behind the wheel of the parked gator, to relax and ponder King's maid. Admittedly, he knew he had been hard on her. When Meagan protected and defended him, he was riddled with guilt, and his indigestion flared up. Jack considered himself a good judge of character. He had the beauty-queen-maid pegged as a money-grabbing wench. His judgment was clearly off. She had shown she was not a money-grabber or a wench, but more of a goddess-badass-vigilante; he had never met one of those before. He enjoyed the last gulp of the expensive, silky bourbon as it hit his gut then headed back inside for the evening news.

Brenda tapped softly on the bathroom door. "Meagan, dear, can I show you something?"

The door opened slowly and Meagan emerged, her eyes puffy and red. "I'm sorry I brought trouble to your home."

"Don't worry, dear. See this room?" Brenda asked leading Meagan by the elbow. "It's yours. The year after King was born; we brought Mattie into the world. She lived four months. We had four months of joy before she left us. I imagine she would have been a lot like you. I hope you will move in with us. You need a safe place, far away from Andrew."

Suppressing the urge to cry again, Meagan looked around the delicate room and hugged Brenda. "Thank you. I love it, but I have my own place. The water pipe will be fixed tomorrow, and I'll go back."

Down the hall, King listened to the conversation with disgust. His mother had basically adopted him a sister in the last hour. The thoughts he'd been entertaining about

Meagan were not brotherly by any stretch of the imagination.

On his bedroom floor, he cranked out one hundred push-ups; pushing out the evening's frustrations. King was relieved Meagan's stay was only for one night, despite his mother's efforts to convince Meagan to move into his house. As he processed the fact that he almost had a sister bestowed on him, he worried about his mother. Maybe she was aging faster than he cared to admit and her mind was slipping. His bicep muscles burned with the one-hundredth push-up. He jumped in the shower, dismissing the intruding thoughts of dancing cheek to cheek with his overnight guest.

Brenda leaned in close to Meagan's ear. "Would you take me to run an errand tomorrow before you go home? Jack will be at the shop."

"Anything serious?" Meagan asked.

"Maybe not," Brenda replied, with a wink. "We'll see."

19 Travesty

King's manager, Marty, was already at work when he arrived. "How's it goin' King?"

"The condensed version is: My life is not my own, Marty," replied King dryly as he poured them each a cup of coffee. "When I'm up here at the shop, I'm worried about everything at the house. Two men were shot in my kitchen and my mom sprained her ankle. I'm behind on finishing my addition and shearing my alpacas. I haven't seen Storm in days, and Dad fired my maid. I hired her back though ... you know, the usual stuff. How about you? How's your wife?"

"Damn, King," Marty agreed, "that's a lot of shit goin' on there! Noreen wants another kid."

"Marty, how old is your wife?" King wondered, he knew Marty was at least sixty.

"Fifty-one; I told her it wasn't a good idea. I think I got her talked into a dog," he confided hopefully. "You know she loves Storm as much as I do."

King scowled. "That's nice, but you're not getting my dog—just so we're clear."

"Yeah, I'll figure something out," Marty responded sadly.

Customers began trickling into the shop and King's day was in full swing before ten thirty in the morning.

He didn't sleep well the night before with Meagan down the hall in Mattie's room. Instead of counting sheep, King wondered what she was wearing for pajamas; he probably should have offered her a t-shirt or something, but he didn't. Knowing that she was wearing something of his—with probably nothing underneath—would have driven him batty. When he passed by her bedroom that morning at five-thirty, the door was open and she wasn't in the room. He found her in the kitchen. She had already made coffee, set the table, and was flipping banana pancakes when she noticed him.

"I can do more than herd alpacas," she said with a smile. She knew better than to give him more than a quick glance; her deodorant would not have held up under the pressure. She couldn't very well fan her armpits with him standing there, brooding.

Amused by her mood, King pursed his lips and nodded. "We'll see. Excuse me," he said reaching past her to the spice rack. He sprinkled a bit more cinnamon into her pancake batter. "I like things spicy," he informed her.

She couldn't look him in the eyes. "What do you mean by 'we'll see'?" Meagan asked, but King was already out the door and driving the gator out to the main corral, He was happy to check on the animals, and breathe, before enjoying her cooking. If he had stayed in the kitchen next to her for five more minutes, he was sure his clothes would have caught fire. "What the heck is wrong with me? I thought I was going to burn up in there!" he told Nosy Girl. "Meagan makes my blood boil. What do you think, Nosy Girl? Do you think she feels the same? How will I even know?" Since he would never, ever, make the first move; King had a real dilemma.

"The pancakes are delicious," Brenda commented, looking over at King, "aren't they? I c-can taste cinnamon!"

He grinned and winked at Meagan. "Don't look at me, Meagan cooked this morning."

When Jack and Brenda glanced at Meagan, her face turned a brilliant shade of crimson, which pleased King to no end. Maybe that was a sign that she was on fire too? He couldn't be sure.

The men shuffled out the door to work shortly after their morning meal. Meagan could sense Brenda's tension regarding her plan to run errands. "Are we still running errands this morning?"

Brenda assured her, "Absolutely. It has to be done."

Whatever Brenda thought had to be done, had such an air of mystery and secrecy, Meagan knew not to ask any questions... yet.

In the truck, Brenda confirmed the address and the ladies drove thirty minutes into town to The Allegiant Community; home for the elderly. Georgia Grand Magnolia trees lined both sides of the wide circular driveway of the magnificent property. Meagan and Brenda gawked like tourists at the sailboats on the sparkling blue waters of Lake Hast, which edged the Allegiant. The sprawling one-story, Chicago brick building, with its tall, narrow windows, was beautifully landscaped like an English country castle. Rose bushes were beginning to flower, daffodils bloomed, and ivy ground cover was sneaking its way up the side of the building near the entrance.

"I remember charting out the cost of this place for her. She knew thirty years ago, that she wanted to live here...eventually. Maydelle was adamant about not living under her children's roof," Brenda disclosed as they stepped into the grand foyer.

A staff worker was pushing the wheelchair of a crumpled little woman with mischievous, twinkling brown eyes. She immediately recognized Brenda. "I know you! How are you Brenda? I was so shocked to get your call, but I'm glad! What did you do?" Maydelle asked pointing to Brenda's boot brace.

"I hurt my ankle at King's house, but I'm healing and fine, Maydelle. This is my friend, Meagan. Meagan, this is my dear friend and past client, Mrs. Sabeth. I just hoped we could talk for a few minutes. Meagan, could you give us a few moments alone?"

"Of course. It looks like they have a coffee bar. I'll wait there. Nice to meet you, Ms. Maydelle."

Maydelle Sabeth smiled prettily, "You as well, dear."

"Minutes may be all I have, according to my son! Now, Jesus—I think He has another plan for me because I feel better than an eighty-two-year old woman should! To what do I owe the pleasure of your visit?"

Brenda got right to her point. "Maydelle, what can you tell me about the Adamson family, and please don't hold back."

"I'm not familiar with that family," she replied slowly; her brow furrowed. "I'm sorry. Why exactly do you ask?" Maydelle inquired.

Brenda chose her words carefully, "There is a girl, Gayla Adamson. She believes, mistakenly, that King is her boyfriend. It's terrible for him. She's very aggressive."

"Oh, now, wait a minute. I do know a Gayla. She's the same age as my grandson, I believe," Maydelle began. "And, yes, she is strange, on that I will agree. She has a child. I never learned the name or the child's gender—such a travesty. That grandson of mine got the girl pregnant years ago and refused to accept responsibility. Not long ago, I guilted my daughter in law into telling me the mother's name. I only know that, because of Gayla, my son bilked me for forty thousand dollars to pay the young woman off. He paid her so my grandson, Conroy, would not be saddled with the child. Not a day goes by that I don't think about that baby."

Brenda detected deep sadness in Maydelle's intelligent eyes and reached out to hold her hand. "Thank you for sharing this information. May I come and visit you again soon? Do you mind?"

"Not at all, you come anytime, Brenda," Maydelle replied. "I don't stand anymore, so you'll have to come down to my level so I can hug you."

As Brenda prepared to leave, an attendant approached to wheel Maydelle back to her room. Meagan appeared, right on time.

"Where to now?" she smiled at Brenda. "This has been interesting so far, Ms. Brenda. This place is beautiful and they have the best cappuccino!"

"Well good! We need to do some spying, dear. While Gayla is at work, you need to get in that house and take movies or photos of that boy, Gary. Movies would be best."

"Hmm. What house? What boy?" Meagan suspected this assignment affected King somehow, since it involved Gayla, which was unsettling. They rode back to the ranch silently. It was apparent Brenda was thinking, or plotting, and Meagan smelled trouble. The last thing she wanted was Jack Pullman on her case for being irresponsible again, but she would do anything Brenda asked her to do, so she jumped right in. "How old is the boy?"

"Twelve." Brenda knew better than to say anything more about the child. If her suspicions were correct, several people would be shocked, but more importantly, things would be made right. She would not tell Jack until she had the proof, and she planned to get it... with Meagan's help.

She and Meagan discussed ways to execute the task of capturing time with the boy, Gary. She became insistent about the need for a video recording. "Veterinary clinics are open on the weekend, right? Gayla works on Saturday, so today may work."

"I think you're right," Meagan responded slowly. Her swirling thoughts were echoes of King's voice telling

Gayla she needed to work more. She might not be at work and she could very well catch Meagan, which would be horrible, but ... for Ms. Brenda, Meagan would give it a try. It seemed to Meagan that it would require acting skills that she did not possess. "You know, I can't act," she confessed.

"It would be better if you didn't. Just be yourself and get that boy on film. You can do it. You'll be great! Maydelle will love you for it!"

Meagan felt taller...if that was possible. Just being in Brenda's company empowered her. Yes, Ms. Brenda had quickly become one of the nicest people Meagan had ever met, other than her own parents.

The ladies arrived at the ranch with a burn to execute their plan for Maydelle. Brenda was too anxious to take a nap and Meagan wanted the ordeal over with, so she traipsed to the main corral with a rope to leash Nosy Girl. She planned to take her for a walk across the east pasture to the rear of the Adamson property, nearly a mile away.

The weather was brisk, but the sun was still high in the sky when Meagan came upon the dilapidated wood, split rail fencing which bordered the Adamson place. She casually gave Nosy Girl some attention and a good neck scratch as she surveyed what she could see of the property. A car stopped far ahead on the main road and a boy skipped out toward Gayla's house. "Thanks, Dr. Lou," he shouted happily to the driver of the car.

Before Meagan could panic about knocking on the front door of the house, the boy spotted her. He froze then changed his direction, and following his curiosity, he ran at top speed toward Meagan. He could not ignore the strange huge creature at her side.

"Is that a sheep or something?" he quizzed, dropping his backpack in the dirt.

Meagan could not believe her luck; angels were surely overseeing this mission of Brenda's. She whipped out her phone and began recording as subtly as she could. "No, she's an alpaca. Typically, they are not very friendly however, this girl is easy going, which is why I walk her," Meagan answered.

"I'm going to pet her, like you're doing," he stated, reaching to feel Nosy Girl's long neck. He was promptly rewarded with a long, sloppy tongue along the side of his sweet face. "Her name should be tongue-thrasher!" he decided, as he wiped his face. Meagan kept recording. "What's your name?" he asked.

"I'm Ms. Morris, what's your name?"

"My name is Gary Adamson. I don't have a dad, just an uncle and a grandma, and she's sick."

"Oh," Meagan empathized, keenly aware that he didn't mention he had a mother. "Why is she sick?"

"She says she's heartsick and takes pills. She cries a lot too." His mood became somber, then changed quickly, "Hey, can this el paca learn a trick, like a dog?"

"I don't know, she's pretty stubborn. Gary, I have to get back to my house. Can we talk again sometime?"

"Sure." He shrugged his shoulders. "If you're out here, we can talk."

"Ok, then, bye!"

Meagan steered Nosy Girl west for the hike back to the main corral. She stopped cold in her tracks for a moment. "Why didn't I think of this—that's probably King's child," she confided to Nosy Girl. Meagan's feet suddenly weighed a hundred pounds each, making each step a strain. As she reviewed the words she had heard exchanged between Gayla and King, she derided herself for not considering the possibility that they had a child together. There was a contradiction however, because the man Meagan had been learning about over the past two weeks seemed unlikely to abandon his own. "Hmmm." She picked up her pace.

With Nosy Girl back in the pen, Meagan met Brenda at the back door of King's house.

"You were gone so long, I was worried," Brenda admitted rubbing her hands together like the temperature was freezing.

Uncertain as to exactly what Brenda hoped would be captured on the video; Meagan played it and commented, "He's a sweet boy."

Brenda nearly collapsed in her walker. Meagan quickly wrapped an arm around the weak, shaking woman. "We have to go back to Maydelle, Meagan. Can we go now?" she begged. "Maydelle was right; this is a travesty!"

"Of course, Ms. Brenda. Let's go."

20 Big Surprise

Maydelle was intrigued. She hadn't seen Brenda in several years and when she stopped in to visit this morning, it was to talk about the child. The child that her grandson, Conroy, wrote off for reasons she wasn't privy to. She was told so very little about the circumstances surrounding the matter. When her son asked her for money to silence Gayla, Maydelle was heartbroken. Somewhere out there in the world, was her great-grandchild, her blood. The past twelve years had been the hardest in her life. She knew if she fought her son on the matter of the money, she might lose him... and Conroy. She also knew if she argued and insisted on information, she would lose them.

Since the time Maydelle had spent with her family was already scarce, any less would have been too painful. She handed the money to Ron and kept her mouth shut about the baby.

She had discussed the withdrawal with Brenda and the ladies agreed about which account it should come out of. When Brenda had asked the nature of the expenditure, Maydelle had only told her. "It's for a girl. I'm helping her get her life on track. I want to keep this between us, Brenda. It's painful and that's all I can say."

Brenda had always enjoyed sleuthing stories and mystery novels intrigued her, but she did not enjoy Maydelle's secret. Oh, she kept it alright; she never told a soul—not even Jack. There were times, over the years when she would revisit Maydelle's words, and dismiss the thoughts, out of respect for Mrs. Sabeth. But, now that it seemed Maydelle's mystery was impacting King negatively, it had to be addressed. Brenda would not stand by and watch anyone hurt her son.

Her attendant stood at her service while she waited in the foyer for Brenda. When her old friend called a second time that day, Maydelle thought Brenda's tone was off. She seemed worried about something and requested another visit that afternoon; it couldn't wait.

"Maydelle, thank you for seeing me again today," Brenda said gratefully. "This is so important. Meagan has a video I want you to see."

Meagan started the recording and handed the phone to Maydelle. The moment Maydelle laid eyes on Gary, her mouth dropped open in shock. "That's, that's... oh my good God in heaven above! Bring him to me, please!" Her eyes filled with tears as she begged Brenda to bring the boy to her. "Please, can you get him, now?"

The sun would be going down soon, but Meagan calculated that she could whip over to the Adamson house, somehow, and get the boy before Gayla closed her business for the day.

"It's really up to Meagan. Can you do it?" Brenda asked.

Maydelle interrupted. "Let me tell you something, young woman," she spoke to Meagan, "I have loved that little boy since I learned of his existence. Now I see that he is Sabeth through and through. Looking at his face, I see my eyes and Mr. Sabeth's smile, God rest his soul. I realize I'm asking a lot, but will you bring him to me, please? I may not live much longer." She beamed tenderly at Meagan.

"Did you just play the 'age card'?" Meagan laughingly accused her. "I knew I was going to get him before you said anything. Ms. Brenda, why don't you stay here with Mrs. Sabeth? I'll be back as soon as I can."

Brenda nodded in agreement. As Meagan attempted to put together some sort of action plan to get the child, Maydelle was on her phone, arranging a meeting. She instructed her son, Ron, and his wife, Karen, and her grandson, Conroy, to be at an emergency meeting at her retirement home in one hour.

Brenda was not familiar with this side of Maydelle. As her financial planner, years ago, Maydelle exhibited great understanding and steadfastness in her approach to everything Brenda advised financially. Today, her former client and friend is spirited, short tempered, and demanding; it appeared time had made her cranky.

An Allegiant facility administrator stopped by to greet the ladies. He successfully tempted them to join a bingo game in the common room.

Meagan was racking her brain for ideas—ways she could convince the boy to get in her truck. There were so many things wrong with that scenario; the worst of which was kidnapping. She imagined Jack Pullman gloating to his son, King, and telling him, "See, I told you she was irresponsible."

Meagan grinned and took a deep breath realizing that in that moment, Ms. Brenda and Ms. Sabeth mattered most; Jack was a non-consideration.

On the way to King's house, she called Rhonda for help. The only idea she could think of involved Rhonda and her son. If Rhonda agreed with Meagan's plan, then she would be bringing the boy to the senior center. She parked her Dodge Ram in King's driveway and waited for Rhonda and Alex to arrive.

Meagan checked the time when Rhonda drove up in her white Cadillac sedan.

"You have a lot of explaining to do, my friend. Is this where you work?" Rhonda demanded. When Meagan nodded, Rhonda continued sarcastically, "Could you have picked a place more remote; ah, no."

"You're funny. Look, this is super important. Hi Alex!" Meagan greeted him; amazed at his height. "You are so tall now! Aren't you eleven?"

Alex nodded and smiled shyly. "Do you have horses?" he questioned."

"Ah, no," Meagan explained. "Mr. Pullman raises alpacas. I will show you, but not today. We have a mission."

Rhonda rolled her eyes at the thought of livestock and the stink involved, but listened to Meagan explain the 'mission.'

"Rhonda, you're going to park a block away from the next ranch down the road." She pointed to illustrate the direction. "Alex will go to the door with me and ask if Gary can come out to play and look at the alpacas. With any luck, he'll come. We need to get him in the car with us. He is about to have a huge surprise, but we can't tell him that. Do you think you can convince Gary to hang out with you, Alex?"

Alex replied, "I think so. I'll try."

Rhonda was mystified. "Are we... kind of... kidnapping him? You know, I'm sensing this might be criminal activity. Where, exactly, are we taking him?"

Meagan sucked in a deep breath. "The Allegiant Community for the elderly and we kinda have to hurry." Her lips formed a thin smile. "Thanks for helping. I have a feeling the real criminal activity happened years ago... but we'll find out soon enough. Let's go!"

"What?" Rhonda asked. "Seriously, this does not seem right."

Meagan was out of time and options so she resorted to guilt. "Rhonda, have I ever asked you for anything?"

"No. Oh, no you don't! Meagan Amber Morris, don't even pull that on me! Alex and I will help you deliver the kid to that place. You don't have to guilt me."

"Thanks, you're wonderful," Meagan beamed. Rhonda rolled her eyes and Alex chortled from the back seat.

Rhonda dropped Meagan and Alex off so they could walk several blocks to the Adamson's place. When there wasn't any sign of Gayla's SUV, Meagan knocked on the front door. Gary answered. "Hello, hey, you're the el paco lady!"

"Yes, I am," Meagan said nervously, "and I brought someone who would like to meet you." She shifted her gaze to Alex.

Alex stuck his hand out, very adult-like, and shook Gary's hand. "You want to hang out and maybe see the el pacos?" he asked. "My name is Alex."

Gary lit up like the fourth of July. "I'm Gary. Sure. Gran!" he shouted, and no one answered, "I'm going out to play."

The situation felt like a bank heist to Meagan, as she hustled the boys to Rhonda's car. "Let's have Alex's mom drive us to the alpacas," she suggested, and Gary willingly climbed into Rhonda's compact car with Alex and Meagan.

"Hey, we passed your ranch!" Gary informed them, somewhat panicked at how fast they were cruising away from his home.

Sensing Gary's trauma, Alex explained, "Oh, there's something totally cool in town. You have got to see it... then we'll see the el pacos."

"Okay, cool," Gary responded with a shrug of relief.

Rhonda drove, biting her lip in irritation. She knew nothing about the boy they had just ripped from his home under false pretenses. It was just wrong. Her obsession with her own feelings about the crime was dulled by the boys' conversation in the back seat. They had so much in common; it forced a smile to her lips. Gary volunteered that he didn't have a dad and Alex shared that he didn't know his dad very well because of the divorce. Their choice of subjects was all over the place; from home life to life on other planets. They were having a great time, but Rhonda still planned to give Meagan a piece of her mind—privately and soon.

Then the Allegiant appeared and Rhonda was stunned. "This place is amazing!"

Gary wasn't so impressed. "Hey, how is this place better than pacas, Alex?"

"Well, there's supposed to be a surprise in there for you," he answered.

"Okay. I like surprises. I hope it's a good one!"

Rhonda parked the car overlooking Lake Hast.

Gary added, "A lake is good. Hey, Alex do you know how to fish?"

"No. Do you?"

"Nope, but we should fish some time," Gary suggested.

"I would be glad to show you what I can remember about fishing, guys," Megan offered. "How about we get on with the surprise, and talk about fishing later?"

A cold chill ran down Rhonda's spine at the thought of a hook in a fish's mouth; there was a reason God put restaurants on the earth. Not everyone was made to fish.

The four paraded through the marble-floored foyer to an impeccably decorated reception room. Ornate, massive area rugs graced the floors. Occasional chairs were paired together creating numerous places to sit and visit semi-privately.

In the Promise Room, Ron Sabeth refused to sit. He had had enough of his mother's antics. She claimed she wanted a family meeting. He thought she was ready to dole out some early inheritance gifts. He was wrong. His wife patted his back, trying to calm him. Conroy settled in comfortably on the plush sofa. He alternated between glaring at his phone and staring a hole through his grandmother, Maydelle.

"What are we waiting for exactly?" Conroy asked.

"We already know her financial planner makes house calls, don't we?" Ron snapped, directing his irritation to Brenda Pullman.

Maydelle corrected him, "Oh, pooh, Ronald. Brenda hasn't been my advisor in years; her friendship is what matters to me. Just be patient a few more minutes.

21 He's Your Boss?

Ample leather seating and a big screen television were situated at one end of the Promise Room. The twelve-foot, floor-to-ceiling windows were topped with crisp, blue and yellow striped valances. Sunshine yellow draperies were held open with massive blue rope tassel tiebacks and offered an amazing view of the lake and low mountains. The calming scent of jasmine permeated the air, courtesy of aromatic candles.

"They're here. Come in." Brenda encouraged the four to enter the room as the Sabeth family's curiosity had reached dangerous proportions. "Good job!" she whispered to Meagan as she breezed in. "You did it!"

"Wow, this place is gorgeous," remarked Rhonda.

The ambiance of the elegant room was a wonder to Gary. "Wow, this place is nice! The TV is huge!" he exclaimed. Unaware of the people studying him, he remarked, "It's a good surprise. Can we go now?"

"Hello Gary!" Maydelle said. "Would you like to meet your relatives?"

Suddenly frightened, Gary admitted, "I shouldn't be here. I already have relatives, and they don't know I'm here."

"Oh, son, they will now!" Maydelle reassured him, the genuine tenderness evident in her eyes. "Would you like to meet your father?" She pointed to Conroy.

Rhonda inhaled her shock at the woman's words. Apparently, this meeting was a genuine surprise ... for all of them, based on their expressions. She hugged Alex closer to her as the drama unfolded.

"My ... father? Ah ..."

Conroy didn't move from his spot on the sofa. Gary approached him inquisitively. "Are you really my father?" he wondered. His soft, intelligent brown eyes evaluated the unusual man with the fancy hairdo and the Internet wristwatch. "Do you hate me?" he asked.

Something clamped around Conroy's heart. He was taken aback by the bright-eyed, direct child, and blurted, "No." It was clear someone lied about Gary... for a long time. Conroy looked over at his father. "You want to explain this?" he demanded. "How is this possible, Dad? He seems like... a great kid." Conroy was visibly shaken. The sweet child standing before him racked his mind—until putrid bile inched up his esophagus. He suppressed the urge to vomit. Though empathy had never been Conroy's strong suit, he envisioned Gary's struggle with his identity and it hurt; shamefully. The boy—his boy—Gary, had to face everyone that ever asked about his father— he had to tell them he didn't have one. Conroy was humbled to tears.

"I don't hate you, Gary. Do you hate me?"

Gary shook his head no.

Keenly aware of this family's need to make amends with their past, Brenda suggested, "Meagan, let's go to the coffee area and you can introduce me to your friends."

They left the Sabeths to their affairs.

Ace's Pawn was slow. It was mid-afternoon when a short, curvaceous Hispanic woman strolled in, and extracted a gemstone choker from her pocket. "I might part with this today," she announced.

"Yeah, well, I might take that necklace off your hands, today," Ace told the young woman. "How much do you want for it?" Ace was positive that piece was one that King told him about. It wasn't very often he came across a huge opal on a black velvet choker.

"It means a lot to me," she admitted somberly. "I hate to part with it. It's a real opal, how about two hundred dollars?"

Ace could have hard-balled her, convinced her that the opal was sub-standard and it would be difficult to for him to sell it... but he skipped it. "I'll give one hundred," he stated.

She smiled sweetly. "One fifty and we have a deal."

"You drive a hard bargain. I'll be right back." Ace quickly headed back to his office where his personal cash box was stowed. The shop radio volume was low, which allowed Ace to overhear her excited phone conversation.

"What's next for Apple Orchard movers?" she snickered, "I'm getting one-fifty for the piece."

Still involved in her phone conversation, she strolled around the shop while Ace eavesdropped. "Nah, I like hawking jewelry more," she answered and pocketed her phone.

Her side of the dialogue smacked of dirty, Ace thought. "Here," he said handing her the money for her necklace. The moment she was out the door, he texted King, "Just bought the opal piece you described. You owe me one fifty, bro."

"Great. Thanks. Who pawned it?" asked King.

"Little Hispanic woman in her twenties. She talked on the phone and asked someone what Apple Orchard Movers was doing next."

"Wow. That is ... interesting. Good work. I'll call you later." Everything surrounding Meagan made King's head ache. He refused to speak openly to her about recapturing her belongings; he didn't want to be an accessory to a murder she might commit. He massaged his temples and texted her, "What moving company did you use to move into your apartment?" The suspense was killing him; minutes ticked by.

When Gayla arrived home from work, she called for Gary. He wasn't in his usual spot in front of the computer and when she drilled her mother about it, Gayla discovered she was clueless. Mrs. Adamson had taken one of her 'mood' pills and then took a nap. When Gary shouted to her, she did slowly get up, but by the time she made it to the door, he had gone. She couldn't bring herself to worry—that's why she took the pills. It was nice to never worry and sleep a lot.

"When I looked out the window, he was walking with a tall, blonde woman and another boy," Anette Adamson explained to her irate daughter.

"A tall blonde? Oh no, that bitch. I know who it was. The only amazon that would know about Gary!" Gayla immediately dialed King's number. "King? Your maid kidnapped my son... I mean, our son. What are you going to do about it? Should I call the police?"

"Okay, calm down, Gayla. Let me figure this out," he said. "I'll call you right back." He texted Meagan, "Where are you and do you have Gary? Where is Mom?"

"Allegiant Community and your mom and Gary are here." Meagan replied. "And the mover was Apple Orchard Movers. Why?"

"No special reason." His instinct was spot on. If there were a way he could end the stealing for Meagan, he would do it, privately and without a gun. Lately, in his dreams, she was behind bars and he woke up helpless and distraught.

King texted Gayla Gary's location and assured her he would meet her there. He messaged Jack and Ace simultaneously, to let them know where everyone was, then concentrated on how this rendezvous could explode. "Damn."

Ace responded, "Busy tonight. See you tomorrow. Picking up chicks at a senior center now? LOL."

King was not too surprised when he arrived at the retirement center and Gayla's SUV was already there. That's how she operated—like a bat out of hell. Stepping into the foyer, King's curiosity hit critical mass. Conroy Sabeth was leaning against a hallway wall, crying; leaving Gayla completely disarmed. She stood with her arms crossed, staring at him, speechless. Cruising past the duo, unnoticed, King heard Meagan's laugh as he neared the coffee shop, so he ducked inside to see her. "What is going on?" he asked Meagan directly, while giving his mother a hug.

"Hello King." Brenda returned her son's squeeze.

"Rhonda, Alex, this is my boss, King Pullman. I wouldn't go into the reception room until all the yelling is over." she warned King. "Gary Adamson just met his secret family... and they love him." She beamed at him.

King reached out to shake Alex's hand first. "Good to meet you both," he said.

"Nice to meet you too," Rhonda cooed. "Ah, hang on a sec, Meagan. Did you say he's your boss?" Rhonda could not fathom such an arrangement. "And you work in his house?" she emphasized. The way the hunky man oozed testosterone was unreal to Rhonda. If she worked in his house, she might melt and cease to exist!

King tried to ignore Rhonda's embarrassing comments; he stood and spoke quietly to his mother instead.

"Yes, Rhonda," Meagan snapped, feeling a bit humiliated by Rhonda's questions. "I don't want to be preached at about my choice in jobs, please. Not right now."

"No, yeah, I mean... sure. Later, whatever," Rhonda stumbled over her words as her hormones reacted involuntarily to King's presence. Her imagination took a flying leap into bed with him. "Why don't you sit with us, King?" she invited.

Hearing Rhonda call King by his first name was like fingernails scraping down a chalkboard and Meagan hated it.

King glanced at Meagan for approval to sit next to her at their table and was relieved when Meagan granted him the spot next to her. Alex had questions about alpacas that kept the conversation flowing until Gayla screamed, "No!" from inside the Promise room

Ron and his wife, Karen, shouted, "Yes!" simultaneously and the door to the reception room flew open. Gayla was trying to run away, pulling Gary by the hand.

"Stop! Mom, stop!" Gary shouted. "Stop! I want to tell them something."

She stopped in the middle of the hall for her son. "You better not say you want to live with these people! I told you someday they might try this," she growled.

"I just met them, Mom. I have a great-grandma!" he excitedly informed her, and gave Maydelle a huge grin. "I have another grandma and grandpa, don't I?" he questioned. Ron and Karen nodded enthusiastically and smiled. "But mostly, I have a father and I want to know him! He said he doesn't hate me, Mom!"

After watching Gary interact with Maydelle, then question his biological father about his affections, Ron understood the depth of his mistake when he believed Gayla, and paid her off several weeks after Gary's birth. "How much did you pay that doctor twelve years ago for the diagnosis of Cerebral Hypoxia?" Ron demanded. "Gary is clearly very bright, and you cannot escape your lies. You are caught, guilty of bribery and extortion."

"Oh no! Oh god!" Gayla began to sob and shake. She wiped her eyes and glared at Ron Sabeth. "I guess you want the money back?" she cried, knowing, as every person in the room now knew, Gary never had any 'issues' at birth. He suffered from Strabismus—a lazy eye, which had rectified itself over time; everyone could see that.

Maydelle listened until she had had her fill of the entire mess, then she informed her clan, "Here's what we're going to do. We're not going to sue Gayla. We are going to love our Gary, if it's okay with him?"

His disbelief coupled with amazement, Gary looked at Conroy and eagerly asked, "Can me and Alex go see the el pacos now?"

Conroy shot a glance at Gayla, who elected to say nothing, and replied, "You bet. Ah, where are they?"

From across the hall, King injected, "They're at my place. How about tomorrow in daylight? Maybe your dad can bring you over about two in the afternoon, Gary?"

"Sure," Conroy answered appreciatively. "Tomorrow, at two."

"Absolutely," added Rhonda, which gained her a look from Brenda. The last several hours, Brenda had been attempting to understand the friendship between Meagan and Rhonda. They were so different. Rhonda had impressed Brenda as a hard-working businesswoman, but extremely flirtatious. She appeared desperate for a man; specifically, King. The issue was Brenda could see that King found her as interesting as a buzzard on road kill.

After the Sabeth family tearfully embraced Gary, the group departed, and a whipped-looking Gayla silently ushered her son home. While Brenda said her goodbyes to Maydelle, King texted Jack, "All is well. I'm with Mom and Meagan. Meet us for dinner at Caspian's in fifteen minutes

When King noticed Meagan striding towards Rhonda's car, he panicked. He thought she would join him and his parents for dinner. "Meagan! I can take you back to the house!" he volunteered loudly.

"Well, I was going to go out to eat with Rhonda and Alex," she replied.

Brenda cringed when King shouted, "We're going to Caspian's, why don't you all come with us?"

Meagan answered, "Well ..." at the same moment that Rhonda spouted, "Okay!" then nudged Meagan with her elbow enthusiastically, hissing, "He has to be the hottest man in the world."

In Meagan's mind, random snapshots of King's expressions, and his body, appeared and began to make her perspire. Hearing her life-long friend comment about her boss in a sexual manner was more than uncomfortable. "Yeah, he's nice," Meagan offered. The fact that King had a bossy way about him, well, she'd keep that to herself.

22 Too Much Cleaning

Meagan was exhausted mentally and physically as she parked the brown truck and made her way in the back door of the B & B. Mainly, she was glad the outing to Caspian's was over.

Dinner with the Pullmans, Rhonda, and Alex was pleasant but stressful for Meagan. She got the distinct impression that Brenda disliked Rhonda, which was upsetting. Mr. Pullman kept grunting his disapproval over various comments during the meal. The seating arrangement was strange. King had requested a booth and when Meagan slid in first, Rhonda quickly sidled in next to her. Mrs. Pullman scooted to the bench across from Meagan, which left Mr. Pullman directly across from Rhonda. When Alex went to sit next to Rhonda, she suggested he sit next to Jack Pullman. That left King at the end of the bench, next to Rhonda, where he discussed alpacas with Alex while fending off Rhonda's advances. More than once, Brenda cut her eyes over to her son when Rhonda laid her hand on his arm or his back.

The last thing Meagan expected when she got home was Mrs. Willowby, madder than a wet hen, waiting up for her in the parlor room. "Young lady, where the devil have you been?" Agnes demanded. "Andrew went home yesterday, I'll have you know—with a black eye! That's what he gets for hanging around with you. Answer me!"

Meagan suddenly realized that her arrangement with the Willowbys was on thin ice. "I'm sorry, Aunt. I should have called you...or something."

"That would have been nice, since we had people checking out today, and have more due in tomorrow. You'll have to help me clean tomorrow since you were gone the last two days. We'll start early. I'm tired. Good night!"

"Good night," Meagan returned. She wasn't in the mood to argue with Aunt Agnes. She was still at Caspian's, eating dinner, in her thoughts. Paxton's face appeared and she was reminded of how she and her husband ate dinner together faithfully twice a week whenever he was not deployed. He was always so busy and often preferred to eat out by himself.

She tried to reason with herself. It was probably moments like this that caused people to drink—just to stop the thoughts!

The way Rhonda went on and on about King, she made it clear that she wanted him. With each of her comments about King's appearance or his smooth, deep voice, Meagan felt more confused. King was her boss and she had never thought about crossing that line, which technically made him fair game for Rhonda and that unnerved her. The thought of potentially working as a maid for King and Rhonda, if they became a couple, was too strange to dwell on.

To make matters more awkward, King made a point to invite Meagan to the ranch the next day when Conroy Sabeth brought Gary to see the animals. If he hadn't been insistent, Meagan would not have said yes. It was going to be a long day of intense house cleaning for Agnes, followed by social pressure at the ranch, and she'd rather not deal with the latter. The sooner she could get to bed and fall asleep, the sooner her problems would be behind her. The pipes began to knock and groan in the walls of the old house as Meagan showered. She let the hot water beat the day's stress from her body and tried not to think about how Agnes would complain about it in the morning.

Snuggled between the sheets of her tall, antique bed, Meagan prayed into the darkness, "God, are you there? If you can hear me, please keep me from sweating around King Pullman... and bring my family heirlooms back."

"Hi Meagan, are you going to be ready to go to King's ranch soon? Alex and I are ready and he's super excited!"

"Sorry Rhonda, I'm house cleaning and not close to being done. You guys should probably go since you're ready. I'll see you later."

Rhonda could hear the exhaustion in her voice. "You do realize this is a habit of yours now?" she scolded Meagan impatiently. "Too much cleaning will ruin your social life. See you when you get there."

"Bye."

Aunt Agnes wasn't kidding when she said she was behind on the cleaning; Meagan cleaned non-stop for over five hours before she finally declared victory over the dirt.

In the kitchen, she poured herself a tall glass of water and drank it under her aunt's scrutiny. Early that morning, she sensed Agnes' irritation went deeper than a dusty house.

Meagan asked, "Is everything okay?"

"No. No it's not, Meagan," Agnes admitted. "Andrew said he's not coming back home while you're living here. I'm sorry. You know I hate to choose."

Meagan tamped down her rising panic. She had felt safer on the third floor of the Willowby than anywhere else, but there was no winning a conversation with Aunt Agnes, only survival. Andrew had the higher rank and Meagan knew she was disposable. Ms. Brenda kindly offered her a room, but Meagan thought that she had already pushed her luck with King. She would have to be creative and find a place to live, elsewhere and fast. Rhonda's house had four bedrooms... she would talk to Rhonda about it later. "I understand," she responded meekly to Agnes.

"Thank you, dear. Could you be out by Friday?"

Meagan's eyes widened. "Absolutely." There was no point to arguing; she needed to shower and get to the ranch.

23 The Opal Choker

Gayla was silent and stern-faced when Conroy arrived to pick up Gary. The tension in the air was thick enough to cut with a knife. Ten feet separated them with Gary in the middle. Innocent, smart, and caring, Gary invited his mother to join them on their alpaca field trip. Gayla was in no mood to rub elbows with Conroy Sabeth or the Pullmans, not to mention the whore who had kidnapped her son and started this 'train wreck' family situation.

"You go have fun with your…father," Gayla encouraged Gary. Then she hurried up the stairs to the second floor of the modest home. From the bedroom window on the second floor, through her binoculars, she checked out the activity in King's driveway. No sign of the maid's brown truck and it was after two. She breathed a deep sigh. She wondered what she would have felt compelled to do if Blondie's truck had been there. One thing is for certain, after the talk she overheard between Gary and Grandma Anderson, yesterday, she would not ever want to embarrass her child again. When his grandmother asked him what it had been like to meet those people at the old folk's home, Gary replied, "It was great, but Mom made me scared because she was mean." Until that news, Gayla never imagined herself as mean.

A stabbing pain in her heart kept her from barging over to the Pullmans.

Gary recognized Rhonda's car at Mr. Pullman's house. He was so excited and glad he broke his mom's rule about talking to strangers yesterday. He would never forget meeting his father and grandparents; it was the biggest surprise of his life.

Rhonda and Alex had been sitting at the table in King's kitchen, drinking iced tea, for an hour when Conroy and Gary arrived.

Hi, Mr. Pullman!" shouted Gary as they entered King's house. Brenda was napping in her bedroom, while Jack snoozed in a club chair in the living room; an episode of Bonanza blared on the television.

King and his guests trekked down to the main corral near the barn. Alex and Gary were full of questions, which King did his best to answer.

"Aren't these animals in the 'camelid' family?" inquired Conroy.

King knew Conroy was never much of a biology student, he must have brushed up on alpacas for their outing. "Yes, they are," he replied, "but they are not beasts of burden like camels—they aren't big enough. Would you guys like to help me fetch hay for their fence buckets?"

Alex and Gary beamed with enthusiasm and followed King into the barn while Rhonda milked Conroy for information about King. Anything she could learn about the hot, bearded man, she would take. Like everything else in her life, she studied her subject then dove in, prepared to win.

Meagan was striving for a second wind upon her arrival at the Pullman ranch. She didn't remember the drive as thoughts of her living situation clouded everything else. She paused to knock on King's front door.

Jack answered. "Hi Meagan, come in. The missus and I fell asleep. King and everyone are down at the barn."

"Okay, thanks. Hi Ms. Bren..." Meagan was speechless at the sight of Brenda wearing the ruby rose brooch. It was pinned to her right side, exactly how her mother, Ruby Rose, wore it; high and right.

"Hi dear, you look so beautiful, Meagan. That pink sweater is lovely. I'm sure King will remember it too!"

Meagan's words came out slowly, "Thank you. Lovely brooch. It looks... perfect...on you."

Ace appeared in the foyer like a gust of wind. "I know, I should knock, but I need to talk to King." He was surprised to see his mother wearing the red flower. "Nice flower thing, Mom."

"Thank you, Ace! Your father was going to surprise me with it, but I found it first," she disclosed, with a wink to her red-faced husband.

Earlier, when Jack encountered Brenda in the bathroom admiring the brooch on her lapel, he lost all nerve. He struggled to remember another time in his life when he was responsible for her delight over a gift. "I know I don't surprise you like I should," Jack admitted when she hugged him sweetly. Until that moment, Jack had forgotten he stuffed the ruby brooch in his nightstand drawer with the intention of giving it to King. He figured King wouldn't mind when he saw his mother's delight with it—and all would be forgiven.

"We'll take the gator to the corral," Jack informed Ace. He was pleased when Meagan assisted Brenda to her seat on the all-terrain vehicle.

The mid-afternoon sun mingling with the gentle cool breeze made it the perfect day for a farm outing. As they approached, Ace began to laugh. "Man, these are some freaky sheep!" The terrible shave job King did on some of the animals cracked Ace up. "Where's their crazy shepherd?" he asked, with a grin.

Rhonda whipped her head around to take a good look at the cocky man who was ridiculing King. She locked eyes with Ace for a moment. The intensity of his green-eyed stare reduced her to a puddle of nerves; she quickly averted her gaze. Prickly hairs on the back of her neck stiffened in response to the wild-looking man. If he came her way, she might run for the hills.

Conroy snickered at Ace in his amusement over King. “He’s in the barn with the boys.”

Ace hopped off the gator and marched to the barn. “King, how’s it going?” he asked.

King explained that he researched Apple Orchard Movers and the owner’s brother was in jail for robbing a church in town.

“What are you going to do with the information?” Ace questioned.

King had the moving company’s address and planned to spy on their moving truck. He needed to watch their operation. “They may have something they shouldn’t.” He prayed that Apple Orchard Movers would yield some badly needed answers for him... and Meagan.

“Let me know what you find. Oh, by the way, here’s that opal choker thing. Why are you into jewelry now, King? That’s weird.”

“Thanks Ace. It’s a gift,” he replied, very pleased with himself for obtaining another object of Meagan’s pursuit.

The men strolled out of the barn side by side while Alex and Gary bolted ahead to the corral to tease the animals.

“Who’s the red head?” Ace wondered, as he checked out Rhonda’s curvy, short figure.

“She’s Meagan’s friend.” King didn’t care to elaborate about her. There were moments when she reminded him of Gayla. As they approached the animals, King greeted his mother. His heart rate doubled at the sight of the ruby brooch pinned to her jacket. He remembered Meagan pointing a gun at his chest. Instinctively, he moved to the gator to stand near enough to Megan, that if she did pull a gun, he would rip it from her hands.

There was no denying Meagan's effect on King's rational thought process; everything about her disoriented him. His eyes swept the length of her as she stepped out of the gator. Her silky-smooth hair wisped across King's forearm like caressing fingers...and that pink sweater... The air was suddenly too hot and dense for King to breathe easily.

It appeared Meagan had been shopping. Her faded blue jeans were tucked into new, mid-calf, pink roper boots that matched the pink sweater she wore. He remembered the soft, pink interview sweater very well ... and that short skirt... and those high-heeled shoes...

Content in their vehicle seats, Jack and Brenda reminisced about the ranch; back when they bought the land and built the house King purchased from them. Before King and Ace were old enough to attend school, they were riding horses and fishing, right there on that land. The couple agreed their life had not been easy, but it had been amazing. To see King take over the property and raise livestock pleased them immensely. Jack noticed Brenda dab at her eyes. "You still love this place, don't you?"

Choking back a quiet sob, she nodded her head sorrowfully while Jack rubbed her back. "I'm sorry we didn't hang on to it longer, Brenda. I thought we were ready to move into something less demanding."

Brenda dried her tears, as she was not in the habit of crying over spilt milk. They had sold it. It was done. She would learn to appreciate their garden home in town. "I'm fine," she sighed unconvincingly, "there are just so many memories here ..."

Meagan took a spot at the fence next to Rhonda and they watched Conroy study his son in amazement. Rhonda's country look was something Meagan had never seen before. Her tight skinny jeans were tucked into tall black boots. Because Rhonda was short, the man's flannel shirt she wore was practically a dress. A wide black belt cinched the big shirt in, accentuating her already small waist. The look was quite country. To top it off, her shoulder length, red hair had been teased at the crown and looked like she just crawled out of bed.

King and Ace leaned against the chain link corral fence posts and talked to the boys. Rhonda stood back. She was skittish about the animals, but enjoyed her view of King and the wild man; they had her undivided attention. Although Meagan was talking, Rhonda didn't hear a word. She was lost in her own thoughts surrounding the Pullman men.

Gary had talked to Conroy in the car on the short ride to the King's ranch. Two things were clarified for Conway. He understood Gary believed Gayla was in financial distress, and that Gary loved her very much. Conroy appreciated her position in Gary's life, and wondered how he would fit in. As he observed the boy learning about the animals and asking questions, he felt proud. Being there, on the Pullman property, there was a connection; like a thick thread had just woven him full circle. He intended to make good use of the tie that was binding them. Conroy had quickly become obsessed with righting his wrong.

Alex tapped Gary's shoulder to turn his attention to an old, bush hog tractor, prompting Gary to ask, "Mr. King, may we ride that tractor?"

"No, unfortunately it needs some more work before it's drivable."

"We can have s'mores at the fire pit," Ace announced, pointing to the cluster of evergreens and Adirondack chairs in the distance. The boys were thrilled and high fived each other.

Jack started the engine on the gator to take Brenda back to the house to gather all the items needed for s'mores. Meagan jumped in the back seat. "I'll help," she offered.

After depositing Brenda and Meagan off at the house, Jack headed to the fire pit with lighter fluid and matches. Soon there was a blazing fire in the stone pit. King and Conroy walked across the property with Alex and Gary between them. Ace and Rhonda followed closely behind, making small talk. When they arrived at the bonfire, King told Jack, "I'll go get Meagan and Mom." Not interested in a reply, King slid into the driver's seat of the Gator.

"Where's Mom?" King quizzed Meagan, startling her.

"The bathroom."

In one giant step, he stood directly before her. "Why is my mom wearing your brooch?"

Meagan's face reddened at the thought that King knew all about her secret mission to regain her possessions. "She said Jack gave it to her. Please don't say anything to her, Mr. Pullman, I would like her to have it."

King was speechless as he searched her beautiful blue eyes, trying to gauge her honesty. "That's very kind of you, Ms. Morris." His sudden formality with her name signaled his caution.

"I'm ready," Brenda announced. She emerged from the hallway carrying a stack of old quilts. King loaded the blankets into the Gator and the trio made their way to the fire pit. He had forgotten how chilly it could get sitting outside in the shade of the huge evergreen trees.

"This is awesome!" exclaimed Gary, poking a marshmallow on his metal toasting stick. "Have you done this before, Alex?"

"No, but it's cool!"

Conroy hoped that Gary would not ask him that question. It was in this exact spot that he had a friend tell

King to send Gayla to the barn many years ago. Remorse, thick as sludge, choked him for a moment. He panicked and glanced at Gary's profile; it was Gayla's face he saw. She was smiling at him and telling him it felt fine. If he had only known thirteen years ago, that Gary would be the result of his desperate actions, he would not have given up on Gayla. The memories returned in a flood and Conroy unearthed the reason for his behavior toward his high school crush. It was King; that's why he wanted to mark her as his ... the talk around school was that Gayla was crazy about King. Even though she was socially awkward, she was beautiful and smart. His father did not approve of her, based on hearsay about her homeschooled brother and rumors that her mother killed her father then took drugs to cope with it. Ron Sabeth knew how to steer clear of people with social problems.

Brenda passed graham crackers and chocolate around and everyone indulged.

Ace began to hum a song. "We need some music out here."

"Hey Mom," Alex reported enthusiastically, "My guitar is in the car. She can play good music!" He pointed to Meagan.

Ace's face registered surprise. "Really?" The woman who drove a spiked heel into the top of his foot could play a guitar?

Rhonda stuffed a huge bite of s'mores in her mouth to avoid speaking. Although she was happy to help Meagan win money and gain fans at The Electric Panda, this was too personal. With Ace next to her, she was feeling uncomfortable jealousy. She preferred to be the sole recipient of Ace's attentions. Everyone's eyes were on Rhonda as they waited for the verdict, but she only noticed the sexy, disheveled, younger Pullman.

"Oh, I don't know ..." Meagan began dismissively. "I'm not that good."

"Yeah, probably not," Ace jabbed.

King nearly choked on his beer. "Rhonda, throw me your car keys!" he demanded. "This is happening, right now!" Rhonda jumped to her feet and dug her car keys out of the tiny, tight pocket of her skinny jeans and tossed them to him.

When he returned with the black guitar, Jack Pullman was the most surprised. As a young man, he dabbled in music a bit, but that gene did not surface in either of his boys. He was pleasantly taken aback by Meagan's interest in the guitar and gained new appreciation for her.

"Are you cold?" Ace asked Rhonda. "We have blankets." He handed her a quilt to cover up with. He couldn't keep himself from looking at her. Rhonda struck him as a seductive Scottish maiden; free-spirited and intelligent, with fiery red hair. He would like nothing more than to be captured by her, somehow. An image of the gorgeous, feminine woman in charge made him gulp. For the first time, as Ace wondered what surrendering to a woman would feel like, his hands got clammy and his heart raced. He wanted to impress her, and that wasn't normal Ace behavior. "Can I get you a beer?"

Rhonda smiled warmly. "That would be great, thank you."

Perched on the edge of a weathered Adirondack chaise lounge, Meagan alternated between strumming and picking while thinking of songs.

"Know any Beatles?" King prodded as he recalled her performance at the Electric Panda.

"Yes," she responded. With the sun hiding behind the house and a crisp chill in the air, Meagan sang, "While my Guitar Gently Weeps," by the Beatles. Her cadence was slower than before, and her tone melancholy, edged with pain.

All eyes were on the fire while Meagan poured out her feelings into the song. Only King could not keep his eyes off her. She looked out over the barn and he knew—she was gone again—just like when she sang at that club. Her body and voice were there, but her heart and mind had jumped ship. He thought about what kissing her would be like as he tried to remember the last woman he kissed. It wasn't Gayla. It might have been the last girl he slept with before leaving college. Thoughts of kissing Meagan messed with his heart rate ... and caused discomfort in his jeans. King knew the optimal circumstance would be for Meagan to kiss him, as he had never instigated a romantic kiss in his life. He wasn't about to change. Yes, that was exactly what needed to happen. He would cast his best line and reel her in until she kissed him. Adjusting his seated position, King concentrated on Apple Orchard Movers.

"Last one, buddy," Conroy announced as he poked another marshmallow onto Gary's stick.

Alex aimed his stick at Ace. "Can I have one more too?"

Ace checked with Rhonda and happily stabbed a marshmallow on Alex's stick; anything to get a smile from the auburn-haired lassie. Rhonda was suffering from 'amazing man' confusion. She found Ace's self-assuredness, scruffy face, and sparkling green eyes, very attractive, not to mention his lean, muscular form. What he did to her sensibilities was unbearable—all the moisture had left her mouth. Ace unknowingly sent chill bumps down her spine. As manly and in control as King was, there was no question in Rhonda's mind; Ace was the man for her.

Meagan strummed her last chord.

"Ace," Rhonda asked quietly, "would you like to come over for dinner with Alex and me?"

"I would," he answered, and joined the applause for Meagan.

Jack and Brenda were pleased with their boys and their interesting guests. They had never had live talent around the fire pit and Meagan's guitar skills were wonderful. With an hour a day practice, Jack was confident he would be playing by the fire pit next time King entertained.

"Thank you, Mr. and Mrs. Pullman, I appreciate everything you have done." Conroy placed his hand on Gary's back, indicating it was time to say goodbye. Gary thanked the group for a great time and skipped at Conroy's side all the way to his BMW.

Ace volunteered to walk Rhonda and Alex to her car after she and Meagan promised to get together for lunch next week.

With the fire shovel in hand, King spread sand on the low blaze and mixed it around until it was extinguished. Jack helped Brenda into the gator and drove her the fifty yards to the house. Meagan stayed behind to help King tidy up.

"You're very talented, Meagan," King told her.

"Thanks. I don't play like I used to. There isn't enough time. Do you play an instrument?"

"I wish. Work came first for me," he shared honestly while gathering the fire pit equipment. They began their trek to the house and it occurred to him that he had never walked with a woman like that—just walking and talking. He quickly reviewed a dozen women he could remember and confirmed to himself that he had never taken a walk with any of them. "Thanks for playing. I know everyone enjoyed it."

"My pleasure."

"Is Andrew giving you any more trouble after his knock-down?" King asked in a serious tone.

She took a deep breath. "No. He left, so I haven't see him around." Not sure if she should share the fact that she was being pressured to leave the B&B, she elected to not mention it.

"Well, good."

In the driveway, King deterred her with a question about her back tires. When she hopped out to see what he was talking about, he quickly tossed her opal choker on the passenger seat near a backpack and checked the tires with her. King assured her it was likely a tire manufacturer irregularity that wouldn't be dangerous. He started toward the house and sniffed the air. "We smell like the fire pit," he commented with a grin.

Meagan smiled back, amused and perspiring harder as she imagined him heading for the shower. She never noticed a "pit" smell on him, just the killer fragrance she had come to recognize as King.

With a boyish grin, King patted himself on the back for staying a step ahead of Meagan. He was terribly pleased with himself for recovering the opal choker before she did. In this strange game of 'find the heirloom', he was positive he was in the lead.

24 The Truth

"Mr. Conroy, thanks for a super great time with the alpacas, and I'm glad you're my dad," Gary stated matter-of-factly as he stepped out of Conroy's Cadillac.

"You bet. Please, call me Dad. I'd like to talk to your mom. Is she home?"

"I'll get her!" Gary yelled, already running to the front door. "Mom, Mr. ah, Dad wants to talk to you! I had fun with the 'pacas at the ranch!"

"That's nice dear." Gayla had been crying; her eyes were swollen and red. "What? Talk to me? Oh, okay," she replied, forcing herself to walk outside. Her hands covered her stomach as she tried to prepare for the gut-wrenching news that Conroy surely was going to rip her son out of her life.

Conroy leaned against his car; ankles crossed and arms folded, waiting. His profound elation, coupled with remorse over meeting Gary at the retirement home yesterday had eclipsed Gayla entirely. She was not a priority then. Today was different; his emotions were vacillating between happiness and confusion. Learning the truth and meeting his son, he felt immense joy. Sorrow engulfed him over the years he missed with his flesh and blood and believing the entire time that Gary was brain damaged.

What Conroy didn't expect was the mental torture and misery regarding Gayla. He thought he had wiped out that painful memory for good. At the Allegiant yesterday, when he saw her for the first time since twelfth grade, he couldn't bring himself to be angry that she had rejected him all those years before. Meeting his wonderful son had pierced his impenetrable heart and left him vulnerable to Gayla once more.

After a decent night's sleep and the outing with Gary, Conroy was ready to face the woman approaching him. "Hell, she's sexy and she knows it," he murmured. She was cunning, smart, and based on what Gary said about her, she was obviously loyal to her son. "All good qualities." Could he forgive her for extorting his family with a lie about his son? The jury was still out.

She stopped five feet in front of him and leaned against the huge oak tree beside the sidewalk, mirroring his posture. "What do you want Conroy?"

He craned his head to ensure Gary was not within earshot. "Gayla, I want us to be honest."

"Ha, great, you first, please. This should be interesting. Are you going to take Gary away from me?"

He sighed. "No. I want to revisit the night he was conceived. I would like you to tell me everything you remember. Please?"

"Oh."

"The reason I ask is because you wouldn't talk to me after that night. I wrote you a letter and ... nothing. After a month or so, I was embarrassed and felt like a heel. Then my dad said under no circumstances was I ever to speak to you again. Of course, a couple of years ago, I discovered it was because we had a severely disabled, secret child. I would like your version, please."

Gayla stared at his shoes reflectively and began, "King told me someone wanted to see me down by the barn, so I went walking down there, alone. You came up behind me as I was listening to the karaoke music. You said you had always liked me and that you thought I was smart." She lifted her eyes and looked at Conroy's face, expecting to see him laughing at her.

He was dead serous. "Go on."

"I asked you if you were drunk and you said, 'maybe a little', but I thought it was a lot, at the time. You just stood there behind me, talking to the back of my head and holding my hands. I asked you if you wanted to go for a walk and you said you would, but only if it was somewhere private so you could ... kiss me."

"I remember all that. Keep going."

"We. Ah. We went to the backside of Pullman's barn, where they kept all that hay. It was like a hay cave. We kissed. I remember kissing you a lot. I cut my lip on your braces!" Gayla's fingers touched her lips as the memory came alive.

"Yes." Conroy recalled tasting blood, but he and Gayla were not ready to stop.

She began twisting her fingers and rubbing her hands uncomfortably. "I may have asked you if you would please have sex with me .... But understand that my hormones were raging. No one had ever said things like that to me before. I was very hot and bothered and made a judgment error."

"No. You didn't make a judgment error," Conroy corrected her. "I did. I should not have left you there like that. You were my first love, Gayla, and I was a horny bugger because of you. When I heard Ellis' voice looking for me, I looked down, and there was blood and whatnot all over your legs, I panicked. I didn't want him, or anyone to see you lying on that bale of hay, looking like I hurt you, so I jerked my pants up and ran out, and then I left with Ellis and the guys. I've been sorry ever since."

Abashed, Gayla buried her face in her hands. The fact that she had never believed him, never gave him a chance, was perverse considering what they shared together. If she had truly believed the wonderful things he said to her that night, he would have known his son from day one. The fact was, she wanted to hear those words from King. Her fascination with King Pullman wrecked her logic. "I thought you were lying to me in the barn," she confessed to Conroy.

"Why?"

"Because you were the only person who ever said anything like that to me," Gayla replied softly.

"That's a shame because it was and still is true. You have made a great life for yourself and raised a great kid. I still think you're smart and hot. Will you go out with me?"

Gayla covered her heart with her hand, in preparation for the heart attack she could have at any second. "My life is not that great, Conroy. Business is down and it's been hard. Why would you want to go out with me? Aren't you furious with me?"

"Only if you don't go out with me, to a restaurant, on a date, where there is no hay," he stuttered.

Shaking her head, she grinned at the crazy turn of events, and asked, "When?"

"Tomorrow at seven, I'll pick you up."

25 The Felon

Since King began the second-floor room addition, he was just begging for severe weather. While he was not superstitious, he knew it would be a mistake to drag out finishing the project. Disgusted with his lack of progress, King called an old friend who was a builder—Dale Clements. Per the architect's design for the upstairs room, the elevator contractor would be arriving that day as well.

Hiring a contractor should have been comforting—Dale was one of the best—but King was in a quandary. His need to work upstairs challenged his desire to find answers for Meagan and her belongings. Meagan's trouble won; therefore, he had private detective work to do that day.

A second call to Apple Orchard Moving and King ascertained their moving schedule. He expected it would be a long day, but he hoped his detective work would prove fruitful; something had to give. Meagan looked exhausted when she got to the house that morning. So many things regarding his lovely maid were such a mystery. She had not been forthcoming about her personal items unless under duress. It was clear to King that she was not going to give up the search. Adding to her mystery was the impression King had, that she was hiding other significant secrets. He would get more answers for himself.

His GPS lead him directly to Apple Orchard Moving and, to his surprise; it wasn't a home-based business. It was more of a trucker's repository in a rundown warehouse district. If King's gut was right, then there was a stockpile tucked away in a unit somewhere. He picked up on two drivers pulling an Apple Orchard Mover's truck out of dock number forty; and there was no 'office.'

Through his binoculars, King saw the two men clearly. The driver was a Hispanic man with a ball cap and goatee. The other fellow was heavy, with plenty of angry tattoo art on his neck. As the moving truck left the parking lot, King idled past number forty to see what sort of lock he would be dealing with later that night. With King's assortment of cutting tools, even the shrouded shackle padlock on Apple Orchard's unit would not be a problem.

Both hands gripping the wheel, King vacillated between digging deeper into Meagan's world and going to work at the shop. He headed straight for the B & B to probe –it was long overdue. Any new information he might glean about Meagan would be welcome.

Half a dozen cars filled the front parking lot of the B & B. He was forced to park in the back, where the blue Corvette sat. "And she told me he was gone, hmm." More than a little dismayed by the sight of Andrew's Corvette, King followed a cobblestone path to the oak-stained double front doors and let himself in. "Wow, you're really busy today," he remarked to Agnes Willowby.

She was a roly-poly of a woman with fluffy hair which she tinted yellow. It amused him that she scanned him from head to toe before informing him, "We have several rooms left. That group meeting in the formal dining room is my son and his business partners. Do you need a room?"

King tilted his brown, leather Stetson cowboy hat and turned his back to the dining room to avoid being recognized. The last thing he wanted was a fight with

Andrew. He settled into private detective mode. "Actually, I'm here to ask you about Meagan Morris?"

"Who are you?" she demanded.

"Well, she came to me about a job... at my store and put you down as a reference." The heat of his lie crept up his neck and he regretted having dashed over there in haste. He would hate it if he had unwittingly made things difficult for Meagan.

"Meagan? She's my third or fourth cousin—works hard—she cleans this place pretty good." Agnes craned her head around as though searching for areas Meagan failed to scour. King was disturbed by the news. Meagan cleaned at his house and cared for his mother, then came home to the B & B to knock out more hours of cleaning. "She's moving out on Friday," Agnes continued. "She hasn't said where she's going."

"That's in four days. Why is she moving out?" King questioned.

Agnes glanced toward the commotion in the meeting room, and then smiled at King. "Andrew Willowby will be the new owner next week. He has plans to renovate and needed her room vacant. We're very proud of him."

"I see. Well, congratulations to your family, and thank you for your reference." He tipped his head in her direction with a touch to his hat, smiled and slipped out the door, feeling dreadful. As helpful and kind as Meagan was, King was saddened that Mrs. Willowby couldn't bring herself to help her cousin more. If Meagan were standing before him that very minute, he believed he would have hugged her with appreciation. He wouldn't kiss her, though; that was sacred territory and he was not about to stick his neck out for a kiss. Maybe he would tell her that not everyone is on the take, and then maybe she would hug him. Generally, women liked to hug King whenever the opportunity arose... generally, he was agreeable to the hugs.

Meagan only hugged his mother. That would need to change. All that thinking about Meagan prompted King to check on things at the ranch. "Hi, how's everything?" he texted Meagan.

"Fine. Thank you for my opal choker. Your mom is enjoying Mr. Clements' flirting." Meagan smirked at the thought of Mr. Clements' jokes.

"What do you mean, flirting?" King's blood pressure was on the move and it didn't feel good.

"You know, chatting and being sweet..." she replied. Having to explain 'flirting' to a grown man was a tad odd. Besides, Mr. Pullman should have known the definition; he struck Meagan as an accomplished flirt.

King had never known Dale Clements to be a talker. He was a year or two ahead of King in school and not much of a socialite. "It's probably more for your benefit, Meagan. I think his wife, Arlene, left him a few months back." On purpose, to keep her guessing, he did not admit to returning her choker; he was enjoying the game.

Meagan considered what King had written and remembered how smoothly he handled Andrew when he showed up looking for her, here at the ranch. He knew what to do and she needed some good advice. She replied, "Dale likes cats, bowling, and building houses; and his daughters are in middle school. Do you think I should go out with him?"

There was no way King was going to respond to what felt like Meagan goading him. Of course, she should not go out with Dale, but he wouldn't tell her that for all the alpacas in South America. If there was one thing Jack Pullman taught his boys, it was to keep your cards to yourself, so he elected to ignore her question.

The shop was buzzing with customers, keeping Marty and the two clerks quite busy. Once King had his morning coffee in his hand, his annoyance with Dale's newfound flirting abilities subsided. He reviewed the inventory list, as was his habit. He liked to be prepared for a transaction, so he memorized the items and what the shop paid for them. Nothing said 'sucker' louder than having to check your bottom line, mid-negotiation. Everything looked normal on today's list; a watch, stereo equipment, two leather coats, a drone, a tuba, wedding ring set, golf cart, ivory chess set ... He sipped his coffee and continued reading until he saw the words, 'amber ring.'

"There it is!" he exclaimed, feeling like a kid at Christmas. "This is amazing!"

Curious pawnshop customers looked over at King.

"You look happier than a tick on a fat dog. What is it?" Marty asked.

Grinning from ear to ear, King removed the ring from the display cabinet and slipped it in his pocket and shoved two hundred-dollar bills into the cash drop bag. "Marty," King asked in a low voice, "what did the seller look like?"

"About six feet tall, heavyset, and tattoos on his neck ... lots of them."

"Thanks." Clearly the driver of Apple Orchard Movers had pawned the amber ring; he fit the description perfectly. A flurry of customers required King's attention; he patted his ring pocket and focused on the business at hand. "What can I help you with?" he asked an elderly man.

The gentleman leaned heavily on his cane. "Well, I was robbed, son, and I'm looking for things they took. That's all. The thing I really want to find is my wife's wedding set. God rest her soul." His eyes misted as he looked in the display cabinet.

A lump formed in King's throat. "Well, sir, sometimes those precious items do show up. Do you have a photo of it?

"Well, it's not a photo, but since I had time, I drew it," the gentleman said as he laid a large penciled sketch on the counter.

The ring was on a young woman's finger. Her smooth hands and tapered fingers were wrapped gently around a coffee cup. The artist didn't miss a detail; the fingernails were short and not perfectly manicured. She was a woman who worked with her hands. It was drawn so meticulously that it emanated love as the hands were every bit as lovely as the elegantly set four-carat Marquise diamond wedding set on her finger.

"It's incredible," King admitted, referring to the ring.

"Yes, she was," the man responded. "The only woman I ever loved. God made her just for me ... and I miss her, every minute."

Never, had a piece art so moved King; he snapped a picture of the sketch and asked the man for his name and phone number. If he came across it, he would call the widower to let him know.

"Thank you," he said quietly and shook King's hand.

"You bet Mr. Callen."

King watched the old man leave the shop before he went back to his office and the comfort of his banker's chair. He buried his face in his hands, moaned, and quelled the tears that yearned to flow. The man had made King feel like he didn't know the first thing about caring for someone. And clearly, that meant King didn't know love, which bothered him. He collected himself and vowed to someday be someone who mattered most to a woman, because he didn't want to miss out on love.

Back behind the counter, he assisted customers and his business day zipped by. When he looked up at the antique wall clock, it was four-thirty. "I'm going to take off, Marty. Are you good?"

"Yup, I've got it," Marty replied.

King was pleasantly surprised to see the progress made on the addition. Dale and his crew had completed running the electrical and applied the insulation.

"Nice work, Dale," King complimented him as they shook hands.

"Thanks, King. I appreciate you calling me for this job. Tomorrow we'll throw up some more sheetrock and tape and bed. That's going to be quite the room! How'd you come across Ms. Morris?"

"And there you have it," King mumbled, "damn." Meagan hadn't been taunting King, she was likely asking for King's opinion because Dale showed a keen interest in her. King wanted any discussions involving Dale's preoccupation with Meagan, to disappear. However, if he must talk about her. so be it.

"It's that 'give a felon a job' program," King told him recklessly.

"Oh, wow," Dale commented lamely, with zero enthusiasm. Considering all the lectures he had given his children over the years about not getting 'caught up' with the law; bringing home a felon would have demolished his credibility as a parent. Still, he imagined how lucky he would be to just look at Meagan, daily. He wasn't thinking about marriage. His divorce was still too fresh to consider anything serious.

King continued the lie, "She's on parole and can't leave the county." It was full speed ahead. He was on a roll. Now that he had defamed Meagan, and disappointed Dale, he couldn't stop himself. Like a snowball rolling downhill, King was gaining confidence and momentum.

"Well, I wasn't talking about marriage, King. I was just wondering if she would go to dinner with me ... and maybe go bowling."

The conversation was becoming precarious. "Meagan's case worker might let her go—if she wore an ankle monitor." King cringed listening to himself berate poor Meagan. "You would have to make sure you had no money on you, or jewelry. Not sure it's worth risking your safety over, Dale."

The look on Dale's face told King he had hit a nerve. King felt like he showed up at the house fifty points down in the middle of the fourth quarter and now, miraculously, he was up twenty points with one minute left to play. "She's nice though, and helpful. The whole thing embarrasses her and she doesn't like to talk about it—at all."

Dale scratched his chin. "Yeah, I can understand that. Well, I should go, see you tomorrow. Thanks." The two men shook hands then a frowning Dale and his men left.

Meagan had started dinner and the scent of herb-roasted chicken met him in the foyer. With a spring in his step, King kissed his mother on the cheek and greeted Meagan. "Hi! It smells great. You're staying for dinner, right?"

Meagan met his eyes and smiled appreciatively; wary of his perky expression. "Thank you. It still has to cook for a while if you want to check the 'pacas.'"

He was impressed with her selection from his freezer. Soon, he would have to re-stock it with meat and fish. He would like her input for that shopping trip.

With a quick nod, King was out the door and on the gator, suddenly feeling terrible. When Meagan smiled so appealingly at him, all he could think about was how she would be crushed by the lie he told Dale about her. He reasoned it was all for her safety, but he still felt like a chump.

Several of his alpacas scampered over to the fence to greet him; Nosy Girl was at the front of the pack. Only half the flock was sheared and the wool had already been sold. As soon as he had Meagan's problem addressed, he would set aside time to finish the shearing. He was counting on a successful trip to the warehouse where the Apple Orchard Moving truck was parked. Meagan deserved some peace.

He packed four hanging fence-feeders with hay, replenished both water troughs, and watched the animals eat. Leaning against the railing, King beheld his ranch style home. Through the big, clear windows lining the back, he saw Meagan chatting with his mother and tending to her cooking. "She is so beautiful," he told the animals. "How did I get so lucky?" As he watched, Jack entered the house and kissed Brenda on the cheek, then poured himself a drink. "I want what they have," he continued, "my parents never gave up. They loved each other, hell or high water." He could not recall a time when his parents stayed angry for more than a few hours. There was usually a bouquet of flowers from Dad or an apple pie from Mom as a peace offering, and then normal life resumed. Meagan set a glass of wine down in front of his mother and King's chest constricted. An abnormal ache had plagued him since the evening Andrew showed up for a date with Meagan. The most unusual of visions materialized again. King had never cared a whit about dancing, but he could see himself dancing with Meagan, in the kitchen; it was so real. He held her close and they moved in step. "Huh," he muttered, dislodging the image with a grin and zipped back to the house in the gator.

One drink would be just what King needed to numb the regret he was experiencing over lying to Dale about the woman who had lit a fire in his heart. King kicked off his farm boots in the mudroom. "Animals are fine," he informed his parents and Meagan. "I plan to finish the shearing this weekend."

Meagan dished the food and set the plates on the table. "That should be fun," she responded with a smirk.

"Oh, we have some news, don't we?" Brenda announced with a wink to Meagan. "Meagan is going to live here for a while. She'll be in Mattie's room, if that's okay with you, King?"

Desperate for temporary housing, Meagan added, "I'll be paying rent."

King's appetite crashed. No, it was not all right. His mother was not thinking clearly. "Sure. Why not," he said sarcastically in disbelief that he was going along with this nonsense. The last thing he wanted to do was make Meagan feel unwelcome, but it was a terrible idea. Having Meagan live here as his maid and Brenda's helper, living in his dead baby sister's room, was not what King wanted. He would have to fix the arrangement to suit him; after all, it was his house. "Let me hire some moving help for you," he told her. "Some companies are not trustworthy." He gently combed his hand over his short, groomed beard and studied his lovely lodger.

"King is right," Jack confirmed. "You never know who's moving your stuff. Half those companies don't do background checks."

The lump of food stuck in her esophagus felt like a basketball. Meagan was guilty of knowing absolutely nothing about the moving company she hired last. "Okay, thanks, but I don't have much," she managed. Why she didn't examine moving companies more closely was a mystery to her in hindsight, because it was obviously the smart thing to do. When she owned her home, she recalled vetting plumbing companies before hiring them. Meagan concluded her choice of movers was emotionally driven under financial duress; she was depressed and Apple Orchard Movers was cheap. No one needed to know about that dreary part of her life—it was under wraps.

26 History Repeats

"You seem quite pleased with yourself, Conroy," Gayla noticed.

"I am. You're here. I'm having dinner with a smoking hot woman, who happens to be the mother of my child. What can I say? I'm fortunate," he beamed.

The neurons in Gayla's brain were moving at the speed of light over Conroy's reappearance in her life less than three days ago. The conversation she had with her mother and brother, Garrett, yesterday was humiliating. It wasn't a secret that her business had dropped off in the last couple of years. Conroy perused the menu at the same time Gayla dwelt upon yesterday's heated conversation with her brother.

She only wanted the best education money could buy for her son. Her fear for Gary's future drove her to desperate measures, admittedly. Gayla thought a good parent provided a college education and she was going to do that, no matter the route. Until a couple of years ago, King had been more than willing to give her the money she asked for. Not recently though, things had changed between them, and Gary was growing up so fast.

Infuriated, Garrett had demanded, "You want us to give up trying to get money from the Pullmans? Why? It better be good, because Jim and Ray both got shot over that deal, Gayla! They're still pissed that you never paid them for their efforts."

Gayla responded, "The deal was, they would get a percentage of whatever they could get the Pullman family to cough up. Your friends weren't able to get any cash, so I don't owe them anything. I'm dropping the cause because I have a date with Conroy Sabeth. He's Gary's father, I'm sure the Sabeth family will make sure Gary has the best education money can buy. So, you see, it's all working out! I don't need your buddies."

Garrett was shocked. "Conroy is Gary's father? Damn, Gayla. Conroy Sabeth? Then why did you stalk the Pullmans all these years then?" he questioned. "You're an idiot."

Gayla glared at the floor and refused to answer. Garrett stormed out of the room, disgusted with Gayla's dismissive attitude towards his injured, jailed friends. Mrs. Adamson listened attentively to her children's conversation with her ear against the wall. She knew exactly why her daughter 'stalked' King Pullman and then Ace; because she herself did the exact same thing to a Pullman.

As a young woman, Gayla's mother, Annette, had it bad for Jack Pullman, but it was not to be. Jack was the brightest, best looking man she had ever met, but he had his eye on Brenda Dasher. It took many years for the pain of that unrequited love to fade. There was an attraction exuded by the Pullman men that, Annette believed, they weren't aware they possessed. For years, being near Jack was like a hypnotic drug to Annette, and a painful weapon when he didn't notice her.

After reflecting on Gayla's admission and hearing the nervous anticipation in her daughter's voice, sheer happiness flooded Annette. She dumped her 'mood' pills down the toilet and went for a walk.

"Gayla? Gayla? You–hoo?" Conroy said, laughing. "I hope you don't mind, I ordered the Chilean Sea Bass for you. You were preoccupied and dazed. Mind sharing your daydream?"

"Oh, thank you. I'm flustered and dazed, Conroy. Aren't you?" she popped back. Out of nowhere, a memory of his hair surfaced. His hair was the same thin, silky blonde hair she remembered from that night at the barn. With her legs wrapped tightly around his hips, she ran her fingers through Conroy's hair and touched his square-jawed face.

Feeling exposed, she casually yanked up on the bodice of her dress and quickly sipped the glass of Bordeaux Conroy had ordered for her.

"Hell, yes, Gayla, I was flustered when I met Gary. I'm not flustered with you though. Not now. There are only blue skies ahead... if you and Gary will take a cruise with me?"

Gayla imagined Gary's face when he would hear about the cruise. There was no way she was going to rain on Gary's parade with bad news. "Yes, a cruise sounds great." As far as Gayla knew, Conroy was earnestly interested in getting to know his son so inviting her along was a no brainer. She was positive all those compliments he dished out were to butter her up so she would agree to the cruise.

What harm could there possibly be with going on a cruise with Conroy Sabeth? She hid her shaking hands in her lap. She believed his intentions toward Gary were noble, but her biophysical reactions to this man would suggest otherwise. It dawned on her that she must keep a clear head and scientific mind around Conroy Sabeth, lest she fall for his charisma and be made a fool, again.

"We've got so much to talk about, Gayla. I want you to tell me all about your veterinary practice. Maybe I can help."

Bewildered by his interest in her and curious about the trip, she responded, "Okay. By the way, you didn't mention where we're going on this cruise?"

"Bermuda. You'll love it!"

Gayla had not traveled extensively, but she did know that more than a thousand people had disappeared in the Bermuda Triangle in the past one hundred years.

As she discussed her business with Conroy, she unwittingly picked the cuticles of her left hand until they bled. She was petrified to trust him and panic-stricken not to. Gayla's heart was already racing at the thought of their boat disappearing in the triangle; she struggled for a remedy. It had been a long time, but maybe just one jack-up in the back of her leg would calm her down for the trip—just that once.

27 Guitar and Bag

The past week combined with his stress-load was having a negative effect on King. Meagan wore a new sweater with her jeans. It was a thin, black, fuzzy sweater with a lower neck than the pink one. He thought about it his entire drive to work. He made a mental note to look into purchasing stock in that sweater company.

Meagan had a nice dinner prepared and the table was set, when he returned home from work, but she had gone back to the Willowby.

The fatigue, plus two beers after his meal, was quite relaxing and he fell asleep. His parents didn't wake him to say goodnight either, so he slept soundly.

It was one o'clock in the morning when he woke and prepared for a night of breaking and entering. Quiet as a church mouse, King grabbed his jacket, flashlight, and brand-new bolt cutters. In moments, he was on his way to the warehouse district.

The parking lot was bare, except for a few semi-trucks positioned at loading docks, ready to accept their morning shipments. King backed his pick-up to the mover's warehouse. The unit was hidden from the street by the old, white, twenty-foot long Apple Orchard Moving truck. He removed the bolt cutters from his toolbox. According to the sales clerk, those cutters would slice through the brass body of the padlock on the metal warehouse door like a hot knife through butter.

From his position on the truck bed, he easily accessed the lock and, with two huge scissor motions, the lock snapped in half; King shoved the door up. His flashlight illuminated a walkway down the center of the storage unit. "Amazing," he whispered, astounded by the size of the space. It extended back hundreds of feet and was well organized. He passed a section labeled 'Furniture', and another area with a heading, 'Personal.'

In the personal section, there were a variety of musical instruments, including guitars. But only one guitar brought Meagan to mind; a honey-colored, Martin twelve-string guitar with an amber pick guard. Beyond a shadow of a doubt, it was Meagan's. The initials, 'AM' were carved into the back of the slender mahogany neck. As he turned to leave, a red speed-bag caught his eye. It was lying on a table stacked with sports equipment; 'Happy birthday, Pax' was written on it with magic marker. Standing in the middle of the jammed warehouse, King experienced the ache in his chest again. "You were privileged to have Meagan as your wife," he spoke to the bag as though it were Paxton himself.

"Meagan, it's Christmas for you!" he exclaimed to himself, hustling to his truck cab.

He set the guitar and punching bag on the back seat. A man's voice said, "Well, if it ain't the pawn man!" Whack! A Hispanic man in a ball cap aimed for King's head with a tire iron, but hit the roof of his truck instead. King launched a punch and clipped the man's jaw. The assailant wobbled and swung the tire iron again, striking King's left arm. Something in his arm snapped, skyrocketing his blood pressure. On the third pass of the tire iron, King grabbed it with his right hand, pulled the man close and shoved his knee high into his attacker's chest—cracking his ribs. The man teetered again and swung his fist at King's head, splitting his cheek, and then kicked King in the abdomen. King's left arm was useless, but he held the tire iron as a shield to block the kick and break his assailant's shinbone.

"Damn!" King exclaimed as he wiped away the blood blinding his left eye. He had to get to a hospital. "Do you want me to call the police?" he asked the crying, bleeding man lying on the concrete.

"No. No, don't call the police!" the man begged. "Just take me to the hospital."

King yanked the man off the ground with his good arm and growled, "Get in!"

"Thank you, thank you," he cried in broken English. "I know who you are, Mr. King. You want cash too. I get it. I no tell the boss."

Disgusted and in severe pain, King informed the thief, "The stuff I picked up in your warehouse, you guys stole from my friend."

"Oh, sorry, man. I didn't know! You broke my freaking leg! You gonna pay for it?" he began to scream.

"No," King informed him. "I'm not going to pay for your leg because you broke my damn arm. We're square. Now shut up or I will call the police." He drove, agonizing over the names of the broken bones. "Ulna and Radius," he spouted, proud he paid attention in biology class.

"No, man, my name is Ricky."

"Well, Ricky, why are you a damn criminal?" retorted King.

"I don't want to talk about it, man. I think I'm gonna be sick!"

King slammed on the brakes, reached past Ricky with his right arm and shoved the truck door open. Ricky leaned out and puked. The smell of vomit coupled with King's blood loss was sinking him, fast.

Ricky sat up and wiped his face. "Man, puking is good. I feel good. Man. You don't look so good, but I can't drive so, MAN wake up! Mr. King!" He pushed at King until he roused and put the truck in gear. "I don't want to die out here, man. Let's go. You can do it, Mr. King!"

King had no idea how he got to the hospital, let alone what happened in the next five hours.

The attending physician explained to King that he could not drive home because of the narcotics in his system.

His cell phone sat in his lap while he thought of the list of people he could call for a ride at 5:00 in the morning. Ace would rag on him the entire time, and Jack would lecture him about how he should have shot the sonofabitch instead of fighting him. Impulsively he texted Meagan, "Need ride please, broke arm, Medical South Hospital."

Moments later she returned, "On my way."

"My Meagan is ... is ... coming," King assured the nurse with a lopsided grin and eyes half-shut.

28 Kiss Makes it Better

Medical South Hospital was quiet at five in the morning when Meagan arrived. Her frantic worry turned to amusement when King saw her. "Hey, honey!" he beamed. "Glad you made it."

The nurse pushing his wheelchair noticed the surprise and embarrassment on Megan's face and mentioned that King was on heavy painkillers. "He has a broken forearm and ten stiches in his left cheek. At least he's happy. Many times, painkillers just make them indifferent and sleepy." The nurse gave Meagan the medical care paperwork and follow up appointment info and the ladies stood on either side of King to help him up from the wheelchair to her truck.

"What happened, Mr. Pullman?" Meagan asked.

"No, no, no, no. Meagan, it's King! We can't leave yet," he slurred. "Go to my truck. Over there," he pointed feebly. "Go back. Back seat, honey…" He handed her his keys and closed his eyes.

She unlocked the truck and opened the back door and stood staring. "How?" she whispered. "Where?" Her Uncle Abe's guitar and Pax's speed bag were home. Anxious to hear about her valuables, she quickly moved the items to the back seat of her truck and returned to the driver's seat. King was sound asleep and breathing deeply.

The sun was coming up when Meagan pulled up King's driveway. Jack was just leaving for work. He stopped short, alarmed at the sight of his son in a full arm cast and bandaged face. "What happened?"

"He had an accident, best I can tell," she responded. With King's arm draped over her shoulder, and her arm around his hips, she steadied him. "Are you ready, King?"

"Ready for you ... yes. Ready for you," he blurted incoherently.

Jack smiled and shook his head. "Well, good luck, Meagan. Looks like you've got it under control. I'm heading to work, but call me if you need to."

"Thanks. I will."

"No," blasted King, "not I will. I do. I do. I do..."

Meagan could hear Jack Pullman laughing heartily even after he closed the door of his Hummer.

"Are you hungry?" she asked King.

He faced her briefly and snapped toward her face. "Yeah, I'm gonna eat you up..." he said drowsily.

"Okie dokie. Well then, you can sleep."

She lugged him into the house, directed him to his bed and set his cell phone on the nightstand. "You should sleep it off, King." He lay on the bed and moaned in pain.

Worried, Meagan asked, "What is it? What do you need?"

He whispered very quietly and she moved in close to hear. He whispered again until she was inches from his face, then he tapped his bandaged cheek claiming, "It hurts."

Then he puckered his lips.

Maybe she misunderstood; her boss appeared to need a... kiss. Peering into his honest, dilated eyes, she cautiously questioned him, "You want me to kiss you? Will that help?"

Surprised by his request, she was amused when he nodded his head and puckered again. Hoping that her employer would not remember any of this, Meagan leaned down and pressed her lips very lightly to King's. Her eyes fluttered shut for a moment then she popped up asking, "Is that better?"

His eyes were closed, but King smiled and muttered, "My pants ..."

"Oh, right." She pulled off King's boots and then undid his jeans and slid them down his legs, leaving him in tight, black boxer briefs and a plain white t-shirt. "How's that?" she checked.

He was already asleep, again.

Brenda emerged from her room down the hall as Meagan closed King's door. Red hot embarrassment blotched her face. For Brenda to see Meagan leaving her boss' bedroom really early in the morning...wasn't good. "Good morning, Ms. Brenda. Mr. Pullman broke his arm. He had an accident during the night," she stammered, "and I was helping him into bed. He's on some strong narcotics."

"Oh," responded Brenda, "I wonder what happened?"

"It's hard to tell. He was slurring his words and is in a fog. Sleep is the best thing for him. I'll fix us some breakfast and we can go check on the animals if you're up to it?"

They enjoyed coffee, fruit, and warm sweet rolls before venturing to the main corral. Nosy Girl clamored for Meagan's attention until Brenda maneuvered on her cane to the fence. She was itching to pet the sweet-natured alpaca. "She's delightful!" Brenda commented, petting her soft wool. Nosy girl responded with a sloppy lick over Brenda's right eye.

"She really is."

Meagan's phone buzzed with a text from King; "Need help."

"Brenda, would you mind if I run back to the house? Mr. Pullman needs something. I'll be right back!"

"You go dear. I'll wait. It's a beautiful morning."

"What is it?" Meagan asked entering his room, out of breath; her frustration was rising over leaving Brenda at the corral.

King whispered again until she moved in close and he pointed to his face again. When she rolled her eyes, he closed his, and puckered his lips. This time, his hand pressed lightly on her back as she leaned near. He pulled her closer and stroked her silky hair. He waited for her lips on his. There was only the sound of their breathing when Meagan kissed him gently, at first. For a drugged, half asleep man, his lips were operating just fine, to Meagan's surprise. As their kiss intensified, it was like hurling through outer space. What she tried to brush off as a silly kiss early this morning didn't feel silly now. It felt dangerous and unprecedented and sucked her in like a stray planet being pulled into orbit by the sun—hot and fast.

King pulled away from their kiss, looked longingly at her and reported, "I just need the bathroom."

"What?" she yelped, panicked that she overstepped or misunderstood his request. "Sure. Ah, okay." She put an arm around him and he threw his good arm over her shoulders; clearly still wobbly. At the toilet, he reached in his jockeys for his penis; aware that she was likely looking, but he didn't care. He would have been flattered if she did look.

Since King's arm was trapped in a full-arm cast and sling, Meagan washed his hand for him and ushered him back to bed. She quickly returned to Brenda and was flooded with relief to find her contentedly sitting in the gator, resting.

"Mr. Pullman is fine; just too drugged to walk properly," Megan informed her.

"Oh," Brenda said. "I would like to know how he broke his arm."

"Me too."

They made their way back to the house. Meagan suspected that King's arm was broken in a fight over her guitar and speed bag, which made her feel guilty. Add to that the fact that she kissed her doped-up boss, and she felt like an idiot; a guilty idiot. She hoped he would forgive her.

"I'm going to have a second cup of coffee and work some puzzles," stated Brenda.

"Okay, I'll figure something out for dinner."

King was a planner and a thorough grocery shopper. His deep freeze was stocked for world war three. Meagan reached in down deep and found Mahi fish filets. She selected asparagus from the fridge crisper and decided risotto would be the perfect side dish. It had been a while since she had made a pie, but since his pantry contained all the ingredients she needed for a Key Lime pie, she couldn't stop herself.

While the fish was marinating and the pie was setting up in the fridge, Brenda laid down for her nap. Meagan took this time to bring her guitar and speed bag into the bedroom she would be renting soon. She set about doing some light house cleaning and readied the table for dinner.

Hours later, Jack came through the door, pecked Brenda on the cheek, poured himself a bourbon and coke, and sat down to watch the news with her. "Meagan, dinner smells great! How's King?"

"K ... Mr. Pullman is ... disoriented."

Incredulous, Jack responded, "Hmm. It must have been a heck of an accident. King has never broken a bone before."

That news was unsettling and caused Meagan worse guilt. "Dinner is almost ready. I'll go tell Mr. Pullman," she announced on her way through the living room. Meagan knocked lightly on King's bedroom door before opening it and found him lying there wide-eyed and studying her. "Dinner is ready."

He thought he imagined it, but now that she was standing there, he was sure she kissed him. Had he enticed her? He couldn't remember, but he wanted her lips on his. He closed his eyes and moaned, barely saying, "It hurts." Slowly, he touched the large bandage covering half his head.

When she moved to the side of the bed, he knew, that's what happened earlier. He was certain of it. King whispered, "Hurts," and she advanced like a moth to a flame. He knew he had her. This time he puckered and she pressed her lips to his—no questions asked.

They had pushed away from shore and the kiss had them adrift. Soon there was no land in sight and their breathing was labored. Her sweater felt like a parka and King's skin like a fireplace.

He pulled away gently. "Did you say dinner?"

"What? Yes," she replied discombobulated.

"I'll need my pants," he pointed to his lower extremities; naked except for underwear.

"Oh, yes, sorry."

He was amused by his sexy maid. The living arrangement mess his mother created needed to be rectified, and fast. Over the last hour, King had analyzed his predicament. He believed he had come up with a way to fix it. If it didn't work, nothing would.

Meagan helped him to his feet, pulled his jeans up and fastened them. She was about to walk out of the room ahead of him when he intentionally wobbled and nearly fell.

He yelped in fear and gave her an innocent look. In a flash, she was back by his side with her arm around him and his good arm over her shoulders. He sniffed her hair. "Hmm, you smell great."

"Hmm."

She helped him to his chair and realized King intended for her to stay for dinner again, so she set a place for herself and served up dinner.

"Mahi! Nice," King said smiling. He shook another painkiller from the bottle and popped it in his mouth.

Brenda and Jack were confounded by their ecstatic son. A huge bandage covered most of the left side of his face, but it didn't mask his pleasure. The last time Brenda saw that expression on King's face, he was sixteen and had gotten his first motorcycle. Brenda reminded her husband that King was on hard drugs and Jack nodded in understanding. They soon realized the idiotic, joyful look was not going away.

"What happened son? Can you talk about it?" asked Jack.

"I, ah, slipped off an eight-foot truck dock and landed on my arm. The guy in the warehouse took me to the emergency room." King tried to keep the lie within reason.

"How's the shop?" he asked his dad and Jack was happy to tell several stories involving Mr. Lee and Storm. "They are best friends, those two. Storm takes treats out of Lee's mouth. Damndest thing, that dog is an excellent deterrent for theft."

King felt a twinge of jealousy. He knew what a great dog Storm was, and he wanted him back now that the criminals who tried to extort money from Ace were in jail. More than anything, King wanted his peaceful life back; a life that included Storm and his ranch and a woman who kissed like an angel.

Meagan began to clear the table and Brenda got up to help. Her ankle was healing well; some days she used her cane and other days she relied on her walker. She happily maneuvered the metal contraption into the kitchen to assist Meagan.

The moment had come for King to implement his plan. Meagan leaned in to pick up King's plate. He turned away from his parents and toward her, closed his eyes, and puckered. Meagan froze for a moment but did not take her eyes from King. The man was her boss, and he was doped, but he had also recovered Uncle Abe's guitar and Pax's bag! And, she knew it was him who put the opal choker in her truck. It had to have been. Overwhelmed with appreciation, she kissed him. King was euphoric that his perfect maid seemed to enjoy kissing him.

Nothing else mattered to King or Meagan in that moment; they were both consumed with appreciation and desire for the other. Neither heard Jack clear his throat the first time.

King hoped his mother and father would see that renting a room to his employee was a bad idea, because she liked kissing him, which was a no-no.

Jack smirked and coughed again, but Brenda was aghast. "King!" she yelped in shock.

Meagan jerked away like his lips were hot coals.

"What?" whined King innocently, "she kissed me!"

"She did. I saw it," Jack said.

Meagan groaned, "Oh, no," and returned to cleaning the dishes.

"Oh, leave them be, Brenda. They're old enough to know better," Jack advised.

"No, Jack, this is a problem because she's moving in, in a few days. It's inappropriate, don't you think?" Brenda had grown attached to Meagan and knew she could count on her for anything she needed help with. If King allowed her to kiss him then she could very well lose her valuable helper. She was too familiar with King and Ace's inability to maintain a relationship with a competent woman. Brenda felt sure King would blow it with Meagan and ruin a good thing; then Brenda's angelic helper would be gone.

There should be no kissing, according to Brenda; it was too risky.

Jack shrugged his shoulders and looked at his glowing son. "Brenda, I think you're right. Meagan works here. King," he continued, "you have put your maid in a compromising position because of your actions. You allowed her to kiss you, son. What on earth were you thinking?"

Whatever antiperspirant Meagan had left was failing her. She had never felt so ridiculous; if only King hadn't moaned, his parents would not have known. "I'm sorry ... I thought..." Meagan began trying to explain herself and salvage her job and a place to live. "He said... he said... he felt better ..."

Jack bellowed with laughter, "Really? King, did a kiss from Meagan make you feel better? Ha, ha, ha!"

King's face was as red as Meagan's. His parents' comments reduced him to an awkward teenager. He couldn't recall another time in his life where he felt humiliated and jubilant at the same time. Brenda's hand covered her mouth to hide her amusement as they looked at their guilty, but still beaming son.

When it occurred to Meagan that King played her for kisses, she announced, "I should go now. It's late." She was torn between disgust at his neediness and desire to be helpful to him.

"No! No, Meagan," King said firmly. When he stood up and wobbled, she hurried to his side and put her arm around his hips. "Please stay," he asked gently. "Take me to the corral? Gotta check on my woolies!" he slurred.

Jack and Brenda observed the interaction through the huge kitchen windows facing the acreage. They were speechless at the ignorance of their intelligent son and the beautiful Meagan. "She loves him," Jack said quietly as they watched Meagan help their perfectly fine son into the gator.

"No, he loves her," Brenda contradicted. "That's obvious."

"Hmm."

29 Revenge Dinner

The sun poured out over the ranch, edging out the frost, and King lay on his bed thinking about Meagan. He played her for a fool at the dinner table earlier, hoping his mother would realize Meagan had the hots for him, and therefore she shouldn't be renting a room in his house. In his desperation to have his mother recognize the attraction between him and Meagan—he freaked her out. Now his mother thought Meagan shouldn't live in his house at all. He hadn't thought the plan all the way through, however, because where the hell would she go? King didn't want her renting from him; he would have refused her money anyway. He didn't want her in Mattie's room either. He couldn't say it out loud, but he wanted her in his room. The question that plagued him was, "Why wasn't Meagan throwing herself at him?" The entire situation was gummed up.

His head throbbed and he hadn't felt so exhausted since he had mono in high school. The bright, spring sun could not force him to keep his eyes open and King finally fell into a deep, long, sleep.

Still in yesterday's clothes, Meagan assisted Brenda with her hair as Jack helped himself to coffee, quiche, and fruit. When Brenda was comfortably settled at the table with her breakfast, there was a light knock on the front door. Dale Clements and his building crew had arrived.

"Hi, Meagan," said Dale.

"Hi, can I get you anything, Mr. Clements, cup of coffee?"

"Yes, that would be nice," he replied, following her to the kitchen. He tipped his head to Mrs. Pullman and shook Jack's hand. "How are you this fine morning, sir?"

"Just glad the good Lord saw fit for me to see another day," responded Jack.

Dale accepted the freshly brewed coffee from Meagan. "Mind if we talk?"

Curious, but frustrated that Mr. Clements would pull her away from the Pullmans, she trailed after him to the front porch. "What is it?" she asked.

"Well, I thought about this all night and I don't care ..."

"Pardon me?"

"I don't care that you're a felon. It doesn't bother me that you were sent to prison and I don't even want to know the specifics. I just want you to go out with me."

"What? I mean, how? Who?" Meagan scrambled.

With a sheepish look on his reddened face, Dale confessed, "King let me know because I told him how I wanted to ask you out."

"Oh ... yeah ... my record," she said slowly, gritting her teeth. "Hmm, Mr. Pullman told you about that?" she repeated. "No one was supposed to know." Her hands were clenched in fists and she felt pure fury in her veins that anyone would tell such an outlandish lie. Felons are degenerates—like the ones who robbed her and left her with nothing.

"Well, of course, your boss, King. He told me because he thought it mattered to me. That's all, but it doesn't," he responded encouragingly.

"I'm sorry, Dale. Can I think about it? I should talk to my criminal therapist about you first. Do you mind?" Meagan's skin was burning with her anger. She suspected King viewed her as a criminal ever since he followed her to her Drakeslist meeting and told her not to rob anymore. The gall that man had, to say something like that to Dale... it was unbelievable to her. Unconsciously, her hands balled into tight fists.

"No, no, that's fine. Thanks. Just let me know." He smiled hopefully at her and waved to his guys to follow him into the house to the upstairs addition.

The moment Jack was out the door on his way to work, Meagan asked Brenda, "Would you mind if I ran an errand shortly? I'll be gone about two hours. Also, since I'm sure Mr. Pullman is feeling a lot better today, maybe we could invite Ace and Rhonda to dinner? They seem to get along well."

"Ah, sure." Brenda could see that Meagan was fuming about something. Her face resembled a pot left to boil too long. "Is everything okay?"

"Oh yes. It's going to be great," she replied as she texted Rhonda and Ace an invitation for dinner that tonight.

Rhonda texted back, "Yes, thanks! Mom will babysit Alex."

Ace texted back, "Why?"

"Just dinner together. Thought it would be nice," Meagan explained to Ace. Her phone dinged with a text from King, "Help."

Brenda enjoyed her second cup of the morning and worked her puzzles while Meagan tended to King. She entered his room and asked, "What do you need?"

He started whispering again, as though he'd forgotten how he humiliated her at dinner the night before. Having felt every bit the fool, Meagan remembered the incident all too clearly. He continued to whisper and she moved in for the kiss; completely guarded; the information Dale shared was her catalyst.

Their lips touched. Meagan focused on Dale's words and when she sensed King's arousal, she pulled back first. "I thought you might want a shower before breakfast?"

He searched her eyes, but they were cold. "Oh. Okay, but I'll need your help."

He stood and she reluctantly steadied him as they walked to the bathroom. He grinned at her and pointed to his jockeys and she yanked them briskly down his legs. He had that crazy, happy look on his handsome bearded face again, which Meagan vowed to wipe off.

"All set," she said, helping her naked boss into the stall. He sat down on the shower bench and she casually reached in and cranked the cold water to the max, then she slid the gray glass door shut, fast.

"Hey!" King yelled, hoisting his cast up high to avoid getting water in it. "Meagan?"

She'd already left the bedroom. "Gotta run an errand, we're having company for dinner!" she called back.

With a quick wave to Brenda on her way through the living room, she said, "Call me if you need anything, Ms. Brenda, I won't be gone too long."

"Okay dear." Brenda sincerely hoped the kissing incident at the table hadn't already reached a breaking point between King and Meagan. Brenda was looking forward to Meagan living with them. But the way she was acting, it was hard to tell if Meagan was.

Dale Clements peered out one of the big windows of the addition and waved to her. She mouthed the word, "Bye," in return.

To know that King told such an appalling lie to Dale Clements about her was staggering. She didn't think King was the kind of man to turn on someone for no reason... Had she given him a reason? It was too much to process when she needed to be getting her ducks in a row about the dinner. After picking up the items that would help her 'teach King a lesson in kindness', she bought a pair of white jeans and a spring sweater, then stopped for a few groceries. She was back at the house in less than two hours.

Brenda had fallen asleep in her chair and King was upstairs chatting with Dale about the addition. Meagan unloaded the groceries and hid her secret items in Mattie's room, and began preparing dinner.

"Cooking already?" Brenda asked.

"Yes, it's a special meal. Everything needs to be perfect."

Brenda's eyebrows went up. Last night, King's face was stuck on euphoric, and this morning Meagan was short tempered and had decided to throw a dinner party. She shook her head, glad that she was not in the dating world like her boys. Walking carefully with a cane instead of her walker, Brenda uncorked a bottle of red wine from King's collection and poured herself a glass. The way things had been going lately with her health and her family's perils, she wondered if this is what living in a soap opera felt like.

"You're walking without your walker, again?" Meagan said, impressed at the sight, but a little shocked that Brenda was drinking at two thirty in the afternoon.

Brenda smiled and took a swig of her Cabernet. "Yes, now, maybe I can be more help around here." Together, they dressed the table, and prepared the food. "I don't think I've ever had Beef Wellington!" she remarked, chopping the small potatoes in half.

Meagan set the oven at four-hundred twenty-five degrees and began seasoning the tenderloin before she placed it in the fridge. "I hope you'll like it," Meagan commented. "It's so tasty, especially with Duxelles!"

Brenda looked to the heavens. "Too fancy for me!" She stared wide-eyed at Meagan's skill with the preparation as she tossed mushrooms, onions, and shallots into a skillet then added sautéed butter and cream. After it thickened a bit, she set it aside.

"Now I'm making the pastry the beef will cook in," Meagan announced while Brenda stirred a mixture of potatoes, thyme, rosemary, sage, and garlic in a bowl with plenty of olive oil.

Taking her instructions from Meagan, Brenda put the mixture on a cookie sheet in the oven to bake. She dusted her hands off and enjoyed another relaxing sip of her wine, marveling at Meagan's artistry. "You have such talent, Meagan." Brenda was awed at the way she rolled the browned, seasoned beef and the 'Dux' paste into the pastry then set it in the fridge.

"I hadn't thought of cooking as a talent, but thank you, Ms. Brenda. If you don't mind, I'm going to shower quickly. I've got forty minutes!"

"Go, go, go." Brenda shooed Meagan out of the kitchen and took a seat at the table to enjoy the view of the animals. Something was bothering her eldest son. He was driving the quad around aimlessly, with a broken arm. She suspected the circle driving was because he could only see out of one eye with that bandage covering half his face. She phoned him to remind him to come in and get ready for the fancy dinner Meagan was making.

King did his best to wash and climb into a pair of nice sweat pants. Meagan was busy so he called Brenda in to help him put on a golf shirt. "Thanks, Mom."

"King, something is off with Meagan. I hope she'll be all right."

"I noticed that too," he said somberly.

30 No!

At five-thirty, Ace and Rhonda appeared at the door. Jack flipped through the television channels until he found a nice vintage country music channel to play while they visited.

Meagan hugged Rhonda and extended her hand to Ace. He was skeptical about touching Meagan, even if it was for a handshake, but he didn't want to let Rhonda down, so he shook Meagan's outstretched hand. Ace sensed something was amiss with Meagan; she had a stern look and a confidence in her eyes that wasn't there before. It spooked him and he looked away.

"Thanks for inviting me," Rhonda said appreciatively, "I wasn't sure I'd get a second date with Ace!"

Ace grinned, happy to be thought of as Rhonda's date. He turned to see the bandage on King's face and his arm cast and demanded, "What the hell happened to you?"

"I fell off an eight-foot loading dock," he answered, hugging his brother. He whispered quietly to Ace, "Apple Orchard."

"Oh, wow," Ace muttered, putting the pieces together. "You're lucky. You should have called me." It disturbed Ace that King was alone and got beat up when they had always had each other's back growing up. He decided he would have a long talk with King and patch things up. He liked things better when he and King were a team.

"Hi, glad you could make it," King said to Rhonda as he shook her hand. "Make yourself comfortable."

When Brenda entered the living room, the conversation became livelier and everyone helped themselves to wine and beer. Meagan accepted King's one-armed help as he set the beautiful plates of food on the table. "Wow, Meagan, this is great," he complimented. "Are those walnuts on the salads?"

"Yes. Is that a problem?"

"Nope. I just love a creative woman!"

"Hmm."

As they were seated, King proposed a toast to Meagan, "The most talented woman I have ever met."

Her irritation with his lie to Dale kept her from blushing. "Thank you. That can't be true."

Ace laughed. "Yeah well, it's not much of a compliment—he only knows two women."

"Now, I believe King is right, Ace. Meagan has proven herself to be invaluable," asserted Jack.

Rhonda spoke with a wad of beef in her mouth, "Oh, yes, she is! This is amazing! I know you have always cooked, but this is so... amazing! Where did you learn to cook like this?"

"It's one of the recipes Mr. Willowby was willing to teach me because he needed my help."

Jack, Brenda, and King stayed silent about the subject of the B & B and Meagan's living arrangements. Her move-out of the B&B was still a few days away.

Ace entertained everyone with stories of customers in his shop and the meal progressed quickly. Brenda and Rhonda cleared the dinner dishes from the table and King made coffee.

"So, King," Rhonda asked, "What's that big thing you're building?"

"Yeah," Ace added, "can we see your big thing now... I mean the addition?" he coughed, failing to hide a chuckle.

Brenda gave Ace a stern look and Jack piped up, "Ace, you need to rein it in, son."

"Yeah, rein it in, Ace. I guess I can show you," King replied preparing to lead the group to the stairs. "Are you coming?" he asked Meagan.

"No, go ahead, I'll get dessert ready."

Meagan took the time to duck into the baby's room and slip her surprise on over her clothes. She planned to serve dessert dressed as a prison inmate. Once she had changed into her orange jail uniform, she set the desserts on the table then waited for everyone to finish their tour of the mystery room upstairs.

"Jack, look!" Brenda exclaimed. "You can see the entire back acreage from these windows!"

"King, this room is really three rooms! What will go there?" Rhonda inquired. She pointed to a long counter top beneath a window with views of the driveway and the cows across the street.

Inhaling deeply, King shared, "A kitchen."

Brenda repeated, "A kitchen?"

"What are you doing, King?" Jack asked, perplexed. Hands on his hips, he peered down a cavernous hole in the floor, irritated. "This looks like an elevator shaft?" he questioned.

"It is," King confirmed. "Mom, Dad, this apartment is for you to live in. You can live here permanently, or stay in it when you visit, it's up to you."

Ace whistled. "Damn, King, that's cool."

Rhonda's eyes began to water as she observed Jack and Brenda's reactions. She touched Ace's arm and agreed, "It is cool."

Brenda dabbed at her eyes. "Thank you, King. I don't know what else to say. It's incredible."

Somberly, Jack patted King on the back. "Maybe we should go back downstairs," he suggested. Meagan stood around the corner in the mudroom. She could hear their comments about the beautiful chocolate mousse desserts as everyone gathered around the table.

Then Meagan emerged carrying a tray of condiments for their dessert coffee.

King was stunned; he looked like he'd been slapped.

"Ah, ha!" Ace shouted and pointed to Meagan. "That's hilarious! I wondered if she was a freaking prisoner in this house! This is beginning to make sense." He laughed harder.

"Ace!" Brenda gasped in a scolding tone. She deduced the baggy, carrot-colored jumpsuit was the errand Meagan had to run. Considering this, she hoped Meagan's short temperedness would dissolve with this performance. Perhaps, Meagan had been nervous about this all day.

Meagan nodded her head. "A criminal shouldn't be ashamed of their crimes, right?"

"Oh, God," King muttered. The slap had morphed into a punch in the gut. He was scrambling for a way to salvage a sinking relationship with Meagan now that he knew that she knew. She absolutely knew what he said to Dale. "Damn."

Rhonda was confused. "Meagan, this really isn't funny. Orange was never your color," she snickered. "Seriously, why are you wearing that?"

Her arms crossed, Meagan's lips were pursed. She had no intention of speaking.

King set his coffee spoon down slowly and stood, clearing his throat. "She's wearing this uniform to call me out; aren't you?" he asked, heeding the hurt in her ocean colored eyes.

Too angry to agree with King, she just stared at him. "I made a huge mistake," he started ...

"Not another one!" Ace blurted. "Shit, King, grow up!"

Jack snickered, earning a questionable look from Brenda. "Let him talk," she encouraged.

"Yes, that's what I'm doing, Ace." King directed his words to Meagan. "I'm growing up. The thought of Meagan in anyone's arms but mine drove me over the edge. So, to stop Dale from asking her out, I told him she was a felon."

"Oh no, Brandon King Pullman!" Brenda exclaimed. She rested her hand on Jack's arm; shocked that King could have done something so immature.

King reached his good arm around Meagan's waist and tugged her to his side. He gazed into her hurt eyes. "The reality is," he spoke softly to her, "Meagan is only a felon to me, because she stole my heart."

Rhonda squealed in delight and covered her mouth with her hand.

Meagan gasped at King's unexpected, bleeding-heart honesty. His words... his words were like a soothing balm. She felt herself orbiting with him again. If there were a thousand people in that kitchen, she wouldn't have known, or cared. She was riveted on him and memorizing the feeling of being held.

He continued, "It was stupid. I'm sorry, Meagan. Will you forgive me?"

Jack reached for Brenda's hand and held it on his lap. "Yes, if you'll tell Dale the truth," she ordered softly.

"Hmm. Okay. Meagan, would you like to know exactly what I'm going to tell him?" King grinned.

"No, that's okay; just stick to the truth."

"Wait," Rhonda cried, "I want to know. What are you going to tell Dale?"

King hugged Meagan even closer and subtly smelled her hair. "Hmm. I'm going to tell him, 'Dale, that beautiful woman in my house is not a felon nor is she available to go out with you, because I just asked her to marry me.'"

Rhonda sighed wistfully.

"What?" Ace bolted up from his chair. "Dale's not an idiot. He's gonna ask if she said, yes; you numbskull!"

"What should King tell Dale, Meagan?" Rhonda prodded. She was passionately tuned into the developing soap opera in the kitchen. This was the most romantic marriage proposal Rhonda had ever heard; she wanted to answer for her best friend.

Meagan's face softened and her eyes became dreamy. "Tell him I said, yes."

Amidst the cheering and toasting, King's heart swelled with joy. He planted his lips on hers, kissing Meagan like a lovesick soldier home for Christmas.

Rhonda snapped a picture with her phone.

"You didn't think this one through, son, you're supposed to give her a ring," Jack pointed out.

King had been moving the last gem piece from shirt pockets to pants' pockets waiting for the right moment to give it back to Meagan. He dug in the pocket of his sweat pants and presented her with the ring.

"Will this do temporarily?" he asked, slipping the amber heirloom on her ring finger. "I love you," he whispered in her ear.

"And I love you," Meagan returned the words whole-heartedly.

Brenda couldn't stand it any longer; she erupted, "Does this mean you're staying?"

King answered for her. "Yes, Meagan is staying...but NOT in Mattie's old room." The bandage still covered half his face. Meagan wasn't sure if King was winking at her or suffering eye spasms, but she winked back and returned his smile—that contagious smile. She was bursting with gratitude for him.

"Cheers, Bro." Ace held up his beer to toast in celebration. He leaned in close and whispered loudly to King, "I have a four carat Marquise ring you might want to look at."

The universe was converging again for King, but in a whole new way. "Thanks. Hold it for me, Ace. There's a man I want you to meet."

"Will do," Ace replied and shook King's hand. "Congratulations."

In that surreal moment, with her acquisition of the amber ring, Meagan realized her heirloom family was home and complete. She knew she was home too. This amazing, wonderful family and this man holding her—it was all she could ever ask for. Curious about the addition, she asked, "What's going in upstairs?"

Rhonda and Ace both pointed to Jack and Brenda. "They are!" they replied in unison.

King grinned at Meagan. "I want our kids to know their grandparents."

Jack gulped and stood up. "I need another drink."

"Me too, dear," Brenda said smiling. "Let's toast, to home and family. It's what matters most."

The End.

About the Author

When not writing, Texas suspense and romance author, Helen Bea Kirk enjoys helping her community provide necessary care to shelter dogs, so they can find a forever home. That is just one of the many things that matter to her. As for what matters most ... you'll have to wait and read.

Please leave your review of this story online, thank you.

Join Helen at HB Kirk Publishing. com, and share what matters most to you.

Books by Helen Bea Kirk

What Matters Most
Done Running
Returned To Me
Shepherds' Mayday
The Bachelor of Belmead

CPSIA information can be obtained
at www.ICGtesting.com
Printed in the USA
FSHW01n1828250518
48464FS